"I can't seer

The admission stunned her, although Anna wasn't sure why. She felt the same way, had from the moment she'd first laid eyes on him.

But things had changed between them now. She could sense it. Ben had risked his life to save her, and Anna knew if the situation were reversed, she would have done the same for him. The bond between them was no longer merely a physical attraction, if it had ever been only that. The connection now was deeper, more spiritual and much more complex.

Love at first sight? Anna wasn't convinced she believed in the concept still, but whatever she and Ben had, it wasn't going away. Not in a day. Not in a year. Maybe not ever.

Dear Harlequin Intrigue Reader,

Happy Valentine's Day! We are so pleased you've come back to Harlequin Intrigue for another exciting month of breathtaking romantic suspense.

And our February lineup is sure to please, starting with another installment in Debra Webb's trilogy about the most covert agents around: THE SPECIALISTS. *Her Hidden Truth* is a truly innovative story about what could happen if an undercover agent had a little help from a memory device to ensure her cover. But what if said implant malfunctioned and past, present and future were all mixed up? Fortunately this lucky lady has a very sexy recovery Specialist to extract her from the clutches of a group of dangerous terrorists.

Next we have another title in our TOP SECRET BABIES promotion by Mallory Kane, called *Heir to Secret Memories*. Though a bachelor heir to a family fortune is stricken with amnesia, he can't forget one very beautiful woman. And when she comes to him in desperation to locate her child, he's doubly astonished to find out he is the missing girl's father.

Julie Miller returns to her ongoing series THE TAYLOR CLAN with *The Rookie*. If you go for those younger guys, well, hold on to your hats, because Josh Taylor is one dynamite lawman.

Finally, Amanda Stevens takes up the holiday baton with *Confessions of the Heart*. In this unique story, a woman receives a heart transplant and is inexorably drawn to the original owner's husband. Find out why in this exceptional story.

Enjoy all four!

Sincerely,

Denise O'Sullivan
Associate Senior Editor
Harlequin Intrigue

CONFESSIONS OF THE HEART

AMANDA STEVENS

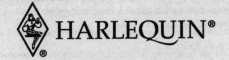

TORONTO • NEW YORK • LONDON
AMSTERDAM • PARIS • SYDNEY • HAMBURG
STOCKHOLM • ATHENS • TOKYO • MILAN • MADRID
PRAGUE • WARSAW • BUDAPEST • AUCKLAND

ISBN 0-373-22700-0

CONFESSIONS OF THE HEART

This edition published by arrangement with Harlequin Books S.A.

® and TM are trademarks of the publisher. Trademarks indicated with ® are registered in the United States Patent and Trademark Office, the Canadian Trade Marks Office and in other countries.

Visit us at www.eHarlequin.com

Printed in U.S.A.

ABOUT THE AUTHOR

Born and raised in a small Southern town, Amanda Stevens frequently draws on memories of her birthplace to create atmospheric settings and casts of eccentric characters. She is the author of over twenty-five novels, the recipient of a Career Achievement award for Romantic/Mystery, and a 1999 RITA® award finalist in the Gothic/Romantic Suspense category. She now resides in Texas with her husband, teenage twins and her cat, Jesse, who also makes frequent appearances in her books.

Books by Amanda Stevens

HARLEQUIN INTRIGUE

373—STRANGER IN PARADISE
388—A BABY'S CRY
397—A MAN OF SECRETS
430—THE SECOND MRS. MALONE
453—THE HERO'S SON*
458—THE BROTHER'S WIFE*
462—THE LONG-LOST HEIR*
489—SOMEBODY'S BABY
511—LOVER, STRANGER
549—THE LITTLEST WITNESS**
553—SECRET ADMIRER**
557—FORBIDDEN LOVER**
581—THE BODYGUARD'S ASSIGNMENT
607—NIGHTTIME GUARDIAN
622—THE INNOCENT†
626—THE TEMPTED†
630—THE FORGIVEN†
650—SECRET SANCTUARY
700—CONFESSIONS OF THE HEART

*The Kingsley Baby
**Gallagher Justice
†Eden's Children

CAST OF CHARACTERS

Anna Sebastian—Lured to San Miguel by someone from her heart donor's past, Anna finds a new life, a new love…and an evil she could never have imagined.

Ben Porter—Can he protect the woman he loves from the evil that nearly destroyed him?

Katherine Sprague—Her heart gave Anna a new life. Will her memory destroy Anna's happiness?

Gwen Draven—She had a love/hate relationship with her sister, Katherine.

Gabriella Sprague—She is the one who found her mother's body. Is she also the one who lured Anna to San Miguel?

Acacia Cortina—An exotic beauty who claims to be descended from Mayan royalty.

Margarete Cortina—An eccentric woman whose strange beliefs have made her an outcast in San Miguel.

Hays Devereaux—Anna's ex-husband and a man with a grudge.

Emily Winsome—Her determination to prove Katherine was murdered could be the death of her.

Chapter One

"Someone knows about me."

Dr. English glanced up from Anna Sebastian's lab reports and gave her a wink. "Not my wife, I hope."

"You aren't married," she reminded him. And despite what his teasing tone seemed to suggest, Anna was not now, nor would she ever be, involved in a torrid love affair with her doctor.

Not that he wasn't torrid love affair material. He was a real heartthrob, in fact, with his dark hair, smoldering eyes and a slow, sexy smile that had sent Anna into a tailspin the first time she'd seen it.

But that was before he'd reached inside her chest and literally ripped out her heart.

Since then she'd become immune to that smile. Nowadays she valued Michael English's expertise as a heart surgeon far more highly than his skills as a lover, although she suspected those skills were considerable.

"Aren't you even the least bit curious about what I said?" she persisted.

"First things first." He gathered up the lab reports

and gave her a look that was now all business. "How've you been feeling?"

"At the moment, like I had a run-in with a vampire." She put a hand to her neck where a bandage covered the small incision made several hours earlier for her heart biopsy.

Michael scribbled something in her file. "Have the mood swings improved since we eliminated the prednisone?"

"What mood swings?"

"Laurel said—"

"Laurel is a born worrier," Anna scoffed. "She thinks if I feel the least bit tired or cranky or if I should—God forbid—cough, I'm experiencing rejection."

He gave her a stern appraisal. "*Have* you experienced any of those symptoms?"

"No." Anna shrugged. "I was just trying to make the point that my stepmother worries too much."

"Any fever?"

"No."

"Diarrhea?"

"No." It seemed a shame to have to discuss something so unpleasant with a man like Michael, but Anna was used to it by now. He'd seen her at her worst and then some.

"Shortness of breath, dizziness, irregular heartbeat?"

"No, no and no." She sighed. "You would think after nearly a year and no major complications, Laurel could relax a bit." She slanted him a glance. "So could you, for that matter."

"Anna." His voice took on the note she didn't like, the doctor to patient one that told her she was in for another lecture. "You can't afford to get complacent just because you've only had one mild episode of rejection. It could still happen. You have to check your vitals on a daily basis. That doesn't change. That's forever. So is taking your medication. Noncompliance is the third-leading cause of rejection."

"I am taking my meds," she insisted.

"You never forget?"

"Not once." The various medications had, thankfully, decreased to a more manageable number from the fifteen in the morning and another fifteen at night she'd been prescribed when she first left the hospital. She still sometimes felt as if she were running a pharmacy out of her medicine cabinet, but she took the pills and the liquids like clockwork every single day. No forgetting. No doubling up on the dosage. Even skipping one time could invite rejection.

Anna knew that only too well. Michael and the rest of her transplant team had hammered it into her head before and after her surgery. She'd had to memorize all her meds, know them by sight and what they were for, before she'd been allowed to leave the hospital.

"Lean forward." Michael blew gently on the stethoscope before placing the warmed instrument against her back, and then he moved it around to her chest. Next he took her pulse, his brows drawing together in concentration as he counted.

He really was a handsome man. It would have been very easy to cross the line from professional to personal, Anna had to admit. He wasn't just easy on the eyes, but was charming and funny and he loved to tease her. She couldn't remember being teased that way since her mother had died of heart failure when Anna was thirteen.

She'd inherited her mother's bad heart, but not her sense of humor. Always prone to a serious disposition, Anna had become even more intense and driven as a teenager, especially after her father remarried. She'd bitterly rebelled against her stepmother and had cut herself off from her family all through college and law school. Not until Anna learned her father was battling lung cancer had she finally taken the first step toward reconciliation.

She was grateful they'd made their peace before he died, but she knew she hadn't given him the one thing he'd wanted most—her acceptance of Laurel. Even in their mutual grief, Anna hadn't been able to warm up to her stepmother.

So it was ironic, she supposed, that Laurel was the one who'd talked her into seeing a doctor when she'd started having dizzy spells, Laurel who'd insisted Anna seek a second opinion when her first cardiologist had sent her home after treating her for an irregular heartbeat.

It was Laurel who moved in and took care of Anna when, several months later, the dizzy spells turned into exhaustion, Laurel who commiserated with her when she had to cut back her caseload at Matthews, Conley and Hart and later, when she had to take an extended leave of absence.

It was Laurel who'd been by Anna's side when she got the news that in the year since her first diagnosis, her heart had taken a complete nosedive, and a transplant was her only hope.

It was Laurel who'd driven her to the hospital when the call had come that a heart had been found for her.

A new heart. A new life. A new Anna.

At least, she was trying for the latter. Facing her own mortality had made her take a long hard look at herself, and Anna had been a little shocked by what she'd found. Her whole adult life had been focused on her career to the exclusion of all else, including friendships, relationships and family.

The decisions she'd made had been brought painfully home to her when Laurel had kept a lonely vigil at the hospital, when only a smattering of cards and letters from well-wishers had been delivered to her apartment. She'd been forced to accept the unpleasant truth that, except for her stepmother—a woman Anna had treated badly for years—no one much cared whether she lived or died.

Of course, the senior partners at Matthews, Conley and Hart had a financial interest in her survival, but if she'd never made it off the operating table, they wouldn't have shed any tears. They would have coldly and analytically gone about the business of minimizing the impact of her demise on the firm, perhaps even finding a way to capitalize on it, just as she would have done if she were in their place.

Her ex-husband had once accused her of being a cold, heartless bitch, and she supposed in a lot of ways she had been.

Michael was taking a blood pressure reading, and

Anna knew better than to say anything until he was through.

"So," he said, returning the pressure cuff to the wall over her bed. "What did you do?"

"What do you mean?"

"You said someone knows about you. What did you do?"

"I think someone from the donor's family knows who I am."

He lifted his brows in surprise. "That's impossible. Both the donor and the recipient's identification are kept anonymous. The surgeons don't even know who the donors are. The OPOs are designed that way."

"I realize that, but I don't know how else to explain the weird things that have been happening to me lately."

He frowned. "What kind of weird things?"

Anna lay silent for a moment. "This is going to make me sound completely paranoid, but I've been getting these phone calls. They always come at night, after I've gone to bed, and they usually wake me up. No one seems to be on the line, but I can hear music playing in the background. You know that tune 'Heart and soul, da-da, da-da, da-da...' Okay, I'm way off key, but you know the one I mean?"

He gave her a strange look. "You say these phone calls always come at night and they wake you up? Are you sure you're not dreaming? You've been through an ordeal, Anna. Both physically and mentally. Your whole life has changed in a matter of months—"

"I know," she broke in. "But that's not it. I'm not

dreaming. I think the phone calls have something to do with my transplant.''

''But even if they do that doesn't mean they're coming from the donor's family,'' Michael argued. ''It could be someone who knows you. Someone with a grudge who's trying to get under your skin a little.''

She'd thought of that. Her aggressive style as a divorce attorney hadn't exactly endeared her to the spouses of her clients, or to some of her own colleagues, for that matter. Still, there was something deeply disturbing and symbolic about the phone calls.

''Look,'' Michael said. ''I don't want you worrying about this. The last thing you need is added stress.''

''I'm not stressed. God knows some days I feel as if I'm almost comatose.'' Anna didn't exactly miss the pressure cooker environment at the law firm, but a year post-op, she knew it was time to either go back to work on a limited basis or find something else to occupy her time. She couldn't exist for the rest of her life in a world of little more than meds, naps and daily walks. She knew of other heart transplant recipients who were climbing mountains. She needed a mountain.

''You're right. It's probably nothing.'' She sat up and swung her legs over the side of the bed. ''I thought I'd mention it, though, in case you want to report a possible security breach to Gift of Life.''

He made a final notation in her file. ''A security breach is highly unlikely.''

''Right.'' Anna knew of computer experts who could hack into the offshore accounts of major banks to search for hidden assets. In the right hands, she doubted the systems at most organ procurement organizations would present much of a challenge.

Michael slipped his pen into the pocket of his lab coat and closed her file. "You're doing great, Anna. Your lab and blood work all look good. You keep this up, and I won't need to see you again for another three months."

He walked to the door, then turned and gave her a stern look. "But I'm serious about the stress. Don't get all worked up about these calls. Unplug your phone at night if you have to. Give it a few days, and whoever this joker is, he'll get tired of his little pranks and move on to something else."

Move on to something else.

That was exactly what Anna was afraid of.

"SORRY YOU HAD TO WAIT so long," she told Laurel a little while later as her stepmother carefully navigated her Lexus through the massive Texas Medical Center parking garage.

Laurel smiled. "Don't be sorry. I know it sounds strange, but I always enjoy coming to the institute. The place is so amazing. Have you seen the Celebration of Hearts exhibit in the museum?"

The Denton A. Cooley Building, which housed the Texas Heart Institute, was indeed a marvel of twenty-first century technology, a state-of-the-art research, education and patient care facility named for one of the pioneers in heart transplant surgery. But Anna's familiarity with the hospital was limited primarily to the eighth floor. "I never made it down to the museum."

"Well, you should make a point to. They have a very impressive art collection, and a lot of Dr. Cooley's personal mementos are on display, as well." Laurel turned to Anna, her green eyes sparkling with exuberance. "I find something new and fascinating every time I go down there."

"I'm glad you weren't bored." Her stepmother's zest for life, for even the mundane, never failed to take Anna by surprise, but she supposed that was one of the things that had attracted her father to the petite blonde in the first place. After all this time, Anna could finally admit that Laurel was a lot like her mother. She wondered how different her life might have been if she'd come to that conclusion years ago.

She'd cut herself off so needlessly from the people who loved her, and it was only in looking back, only with the angel of death knocking at her door, that Anna had come to realize it was fear that drove her. Not ambition, not greed, not even her dislike and resentment of Laurel. Fear that if she cared too much, she might end up losing someone else.

Her mother's death had affected Anna far more than she'd ever been willing to acknowledge, and her father—so much like Anna—had kept his own grief bottled inside. He'd refused to talk about her mother's death, refused to allow Anna to talk about it. They'd both become very good at pretending and hiding their grief from one another. That was why when he'd brought Laurel home, without any warning, Anna had thought it the worst kind of betrayal.

She hadn't been able to forgive him, hadn't wanted any part of their happiness, because by then, she'd found something far more reliable and far less complicated than love. Success. Her professional life was something she had complete control over—or so she'd thought.

Deep in her reverie, Anna stared out the window as they pulled out of the parking garage and merged with traffic on the street. It was raining, and the rhythmic sound of the windshield wipers made her a little drowsy. It was a good thing Laurel was behind the wheel, she decided, resting her head against the back of the seat. Michael had given her the green light to resume driving six weeks after she left the hospital, but on biopsy days, she still had to rely on her stepmother.

Laurel had a few errands to run while they were out, including a stop at the pharmacy to replenish some of Anna's meds, and by the time they finally left the medical center, it was after three and traffic was already congested. As they headed north on Main Street through downtown, Anna impulsively gestured to a parking garage on the left. "Pull in there."

Laurel did as she was told, then flashed Anna a quick frown. "You're not going into the office, I hope."

Matthews, Conley and Hart occupied several floors of the J. P. Morgan Chase Tower, the tallest building in downtown Houston. Anna's office was on the eighty-fifth floor, and on a clear day, she could glimpse the Gulf of Mexico. But Houston was a city at the mercy of a subtropical climate and the belching smokestacks from its dozens of oil refineries. A clear day in the downtown area was something of a rare occurrence.

"Anna," Laurel admonished. "You really should go home and rest."

"This won't take long. Just drop me near the lobby, and then you go on home without me. You've waited enough for one day."

"How will you get home?" Laurel worried.

"I'll walk. I'm up to four miles a day," she said when her stepmother tried to protest. "I think I can handle a few city blocks."

"But it's still raining."

Anna held up her umbrella. "I've got my rain gear, and if it starts coming down harder, I'll take a cab."

Laurel found a place to park, then turned to Anna. "I'm worried about you, Anna. I've noticed how restless and preoccupied you've been lately, and I'm afraid you're going to do something to jeopardize your health."

Anna opened the door. "I have something I need to take care of, but it's nothing for you to worry about. I promise."

She got out of the car before Laurel could argue further and waved her on. Her stepmother hesitated for a moment, her brows drawn together in a deep frown, and then she reluctantly drove off.

From the lobby in the parking garage, Anna took the escalator down into the tunnels, a six-mile subterranean network that connected most of the major buildings in downtown Houston. The tunnels were air-conditioned and well lighted and contained everything from chiropractic clinics to offbeat boutiques, but somehow Anna could never quite conquer the oppressive feeling of being underground.

Hurrying underneath Travis Street, she rode another escalator up to the sleek glass-and-granite lobby of the Chase Tower, and then waited for an elevator to take her to the sixty-seventh floor where the offices of BMI Global Investigations were located.

The bell pinged and the doors slid open. As Anna stood back for the half dozen or so well-dressed professionals to disembark, she noticed a man at the rear of the elevator. He was taller than the other passengers, which might explain why her gaze was drawn to him. But Anna suspected it had more to do with the long, thin scar that ran from the top of his cheekbone to the curve of his chin. She'd finally gotten used to her own scar so the sight didn't put her off, but she couldn't help wondering what had happened to him.

He wasn't dressed in a business suit as all the others were, but wore instead a dark-colored shirt and pants that seemed out of place in Houston on a muggy, rainy afternoon in July. The humidity outside was killer, but the man seemed oblivious to the weather, his fellow passengers and especially to Anna. He barely glanced at her even when they accidentally brushed shoulders as he got off the elevator.

''Excuse me,'' he murmured.

A chill shot up Anna's backbone. She could feel gooseflesh prickling along her bare arms as she was shuffled to the back of the car. Through the crowd, she caught a glimpse of the man moving quickly away.

But just before the doors slid closed, he stopped suddenly and glanced back, his gaze searching the elevator as he lifted a hand to the back of his neck.

BMI WAS A LARGE private investigation firm founded by two former H.P.D. homicide detectives and an ex-FBI special agent who'd worked out of the field office in Houston for over a decade. They now employed over a dozen certified investigators and a specialized support staff that included computer experts and forensic accountants who were masters at ferreting out hidden assets and undisclosed bank accounts, a service Anna had found invaluable over the years.

Matthews, Conley and Hart used the P.I. firm exclusively, and Anna had worked with all three of the principle investigators at one time or another. They each had their talents and areas of expertise, but she felt a little more comfortable with Tom Bellows. He was the oldest of the three, and he'd always secretly reminded her of her father.

The receptionist did a double take when she first saw Anna step through the doorway, and then she gave her a wary greeting. "Hello, Ms. Sebastian. We haven't seen you in quite a while. Do you have an appointment?"

No inquiry as to her health, Anna noticed, but she could hardly blame the girl. Before Anna got sick, she would breeze into the office for a quick consultation with one of the investigators, barely giving whoever was behind the desk the time of day. She was ashamed now to admit that she'd never taken the time to learn the receptionist's name. Nor had she ever noticed how pretty the girl was, with her long, silky hair and crystalline green eyes.

Anna glanced at the brass plate on the corner of the desk and committed the name to memory. "Hello, Juliette. I don't have an appointment, but I really need to see Tom Bellows. Is he in?"

"Hold on and I'll check."

"Thanks." Anna smiled her appreciation, and the receptionist was clearly stunned by her new, cordial demeanor.

When Juliette hung up the phone, she said in a careful voice, "You can go on back. Mr. Bellows has a few minutes before his next appointment." She glanced at Anna, and then quickly looked away, as if she wasn't quite sure how to respond to her.

Anna thanked her again, and then started down the hall to Tom Bellows's office. He was standing in the doorway waiting for her. At fifty-five, he was still a fit and handsome man with silver hair, piercing blue eyes and a tanned, weathered complexion that attested to his passion for deep-sea fishing.

"I thought Juliette had to be mistaken," he said in a serious tone. "But it really is you. Welcome back to the land of the living."

"Thanks." A very apt way of putting it, Anna thought as she followed him into his office. He motioned her to a chair across from his desk and she sat down, draping her raincoat across the arm and placing her red umbrella on the floor beside her.

Tom sat down behind his desk and gave her a long,

frank appraisal. "Last time I saw you, I wasn't sure you were going to make it."

She gave him a wry smile. "A lot's happened since then."

He nodded. "I heard you got the transplant."

"Yes, thanks for the card you sent." Tom's had been one of the few cards that had been waiting for her when she'd gone home from the hospital. It had meant a lot.

He was still studying her with undisguised curiosity. "I may be crazy, but I swear you look different. I can't quite put my finger on what it is."

"I lost quite a bit of weight," she said with a shrug.

"You were always thin. That's not it." He tilted his head. "It's the eyes." He stared at her for a moment longer, and then glanced away suddenly, as if disturbed by something he'd seen. "You've been through a lot. I can see that."

She nodded, suddenly very uncomfortable with the direction the conversation had taken. She cleared her throat. "You're probably wondering why I'm here."

"I assumed you were back at work."

"No. And to be quite honest, I'm not even sure I'm going back."

He lifted a brow in surprise. "They know that upstairs?"

"I haven't handed in my formal resignation, but I suspect they have a pretty good idea. It's been almost a year, after all."

He rubbed his chin. "They'd probably give you another year if you wanted it. An attorney with your abilities and instincts doesn't come along every day."

Abilities as in ambition. Instincts as in sheer, cut-throat ruthlessness. She drew a deep breath. "That was the old Anna."

He smiled. "I'll admit you do seem different, but I've never seen a leopard yet who can change its spots overnight."

"Maybe you haven't seen one whose life depended on it," she countered.

Tom seemed to consider the possibility for a moment. He shuffled some papers on his desk. "Why don't you tell me why you're here?"

"I have a job for you."

"But I thought you said—"

"It's personal."

"All right, I'm listening." But a frown already played between his brows as if he were anticipating something unpleasant.

"I want to find out the identity of my donor."

He glanced up, his frown deepening. "Then why not go through the proper channels? I read somewhere that transplant recipients write an anonymous letter to their donor's family, and it's delivered through the hospital. The family has the choice to either respond or ignore the letter. Eventually, if both sides agree, they can meet face-to-face."

Anna impatiently drummed her fingers on the chair arms. "What if the family decides they don't want to meet me?"

"Then that might be for the best." Tom sat forward, gazing at her intently. He was clearly disturbed by her suggestion. "Look, Anna, I think you're only looking at this thing from one side, but the safeguards are in place for your protection as well as the donor's family. Let me give you an example. What if a bereaved mother finds out you have her son's heart? What if she's had a hard time accepting her son's death? What if she starts calling you in the middle of the night or showing up on your doorstep unexpectedly? I'm not saying anything like that would happen, but it could.''

Apprehension tingled along Anna's nerve endings as she thought about the phone calls. ''I see your point, and I appreciate your concern, Tom. But I think it's possible someone in the donor's family may already know who I am.''

She told him then about the phone calls, and when she finished, he drew the same conclusion as Michael. ''I agree that's pretty strange, but it doesn't mean the calls are coming from someone in the donor's family. A lot of people…know about your transplant.''

She had a feeling what he'd meant to say was that a lot of people had it in for her.

''Your transplant was even mentioned in the paper,'' Tom pointed out. ''So it's hardly a secret.''

Anna nodded. ''My stepmother showed me the article.'' Her name and medical condition had been included in a follow-up piece to a highly publicized trial she'd litigated for the firm. She supposed it was possible that someone she'd crossed swords with in the courtroom, or even in the office, had seen that article as well and had, as Michael said, decided to get under her skin a little. ''I know what you're getting at,'' she told Tom. ''And, yes, I've made a few enemies. But

I honestly don't think that's it. The phone calls are more—''

"Mind sick?" he supplied.

A shiver crawled up Anna's backbone, not unlike the one she'd experienced earlier in the elevator. She thought about the man with the scar, wondering again who had sliced open his face. And why.

She glanced at Tom. "I was going to say personal. It might even be that someone is trying to reach out to me."

"Which is exactly my earlier point," he reminded her grimly.

"Look, even if I knew who was responsible for the calls, it wouldn't change my mind." Anna leaned toward him. "I don't expect you to understand, but this is something I have to do. I know my donor was a thirty-nine-year-old woman, but I need to know what kind of person she was, the kind of life she led. Don't ask me to explain it, but I feel as if I owe her that much."

"Don't you think your gratitude would be better served by honoring her family's privacy?" Tom asked bluntly.

Anna drew a breath. "Are you saying you won't help me?"

He looked away, unable to hold her gaze. "I'm saying I have deep reservations about this. About your motives."

Anger darted through her. She sat back in her chair, eyeing him coldly. "You know, Tom, I'm the one who brought Matthews, Conley and Hart to your firm.

One call and I could just as easily take that business away from you.''

His jaw hardened as he returned her stare. "I'm aware of that.''

Anna was at once struck by remorse. She put a hand to her mouth. "Tom, that was completely out of line. I apologize.''

Tom shrugged, but something had changed between them. Anna could see it in his eyes. "Don't apologize. In some ways, it's a relief to know the real Anna Sebastian is still around.''

He studied her for a moment, as if he couldn't quite decide whether her remorse was genuine or not. "You know, Anna, I've always admired and respected you. I've even at times felt a certain fondness for you. But you've never made it easy for people to care about you.''

"I know that.''

He rubbed the back of his neck. "I'm going to do this for you because you're right. I do owe you. But after that…'' he trailed off on a shrug, and guilt and humiliation welled inside Anna where once she would have allowed herself to feel nothing but anger. Tom was about the closest thing to a friend she had, and now she'd pushed him away. Maybe he was right. Maybe a leopard couldn't change its spots overnight. Maybe she couldn't change them at all.

"If you'd rather I take this to another agency, I'll understand. And there won't be any hard feelings. No…repercussions.''

He shook his head. "I said I'd look into it, and I

will. I just hope you know what you could be letting yourself in for.''

"I do. And I want you to know that I'm not going to hurt anyone with this information. Whatever you find out will stay between us." She paused again. "I know it's hard for you to understand, but this is something I have to do. I have to make sure…"

"You deserve your new heart?"

His insight stunned her. "Yes, exactly," Anna murmured. "And I can tell by your expression what your opinion is on the subject."

"It doesn't matter what I think." He stood, drawing the meeting to an end. "I'll be in touch."

He didn't bother seeing her out.

Chapter Two

Anna felt deeply unsettled as she headed up Travis Street toward her apartment in the old Cullen Bank Building on Main. The weather didn't help. It was after four and the late-afternoon traffic was starting to stack up on the streets, but she was only one of a handful of pedestrians on the sidewalks. The rain had driven everyone else down into the tunnels. Even the terrace at Cabo's, a trendy Mexican restaurant and bar, looked damply forlorn in the drizzle.

Crossing the intersection at Preston, Anna began to experience a strange sensation of being watched. She glanced over her shoulder, saw no one behind her, and continued on toward Congress. She waited for the light, and then crossed the street. As she hurried toward her building, her gaze was inexplicably drawn to the covered bus stop at the corner.

A man stood inside, staring at the slow-moving traffic on Congress. He had his back to Anna, but something about him looked familiar. He was tall, with closely cropped dark hair and broad shoulders beneath a black shirt.

Her stomach fluttered as she stood watching him.

For a moment, she thought he was the man from the elevator, and something told her to run—not walk—away from him. To hurry inside her building, rush up to her ninth-floor apartment and lock the door behind her.

But she couldn't seem to move. And then, as if sensing her scrutiny, he turned slowly to stare at her. Anna caught her breath, realizing at once why he'd seemed familiar to her.

Her ex-husband smiled as he left the shelter of the bus stop and started toward her.

"Hello, Anna."

"Hays," she said in surprise. Her hand had gone automatically to her heart, and now she self-consciously dropped her arm to her side. "What are you doing here?"

"Waiting for you." Moisture glinted in his dark hair. "I saw you getting on the elevator in the Chase Tower, and I tried to catch you, but you didn't go up to your office." He shrugged. "I figured you had to come this way sooner or later."

His excuse sounded a bit convenient to Anna although plausible, she supposed. Hays worked for an oil and gas exploration company headquartered in the Chase Tower, which was how they'd first met.

She decided to play the meeting by ear. "So why did you want to see me?"

"I've been working out of the Dallas office for the past several months, and I just got back in town a few days ago. I heard what happened." His gaze dropped very briefly to her chest. "I guess I needed to see for myself that you were okay."

Anna wanted to accept his concern at face value, but there was something in his eyes that made her say warily, "You didn't have to go to so much trouble. You could have just called."

"Like I said, I needed to see for myself." He stared down at her. "Can I ask you something?"

Anna shrugged. "Sure."

"How does it feel to have someone else's heart beating inside your chest?"

How was she supposed to answer that? Should she tell him she felt an appreciation bordering on reverence for her new heart? That she was deeply humbled by a second chance she'd done nothing to deserve? That she felt an almost spiritual connection with the woman who'd given her the ultimate gift?

She could tell him all those things, but she could never make Hays or anyone else understand if they'd never walked in her shoes.

"It feels just like my own," she said, but that wasn't altogether true.

He cocked his head. "I heard about this guy once. He got a new heart just like you, and he suddenly developed a strange affinity for pasta. Spaghetti, fettuccini, you name it. He never could stand the stuff before, but suddenly he couldn't get enough of it. Turned out his donor had loved Italian food." Hays arched an eyebrow. "How about it, Anna? Had any strange cravings since your surgery?"

"Not that I've noticed."

"What, no new abilities or talents?"

"No." She shivered a bit in the light rain. "But…I have changed."

One brow shot up again. "How so?"

She hesitated, unsure how to phrase what she wanted to say, but more important, not certain how he would take it. "I'm glad you came here to wait for me, Hays, because there's something I've wanted to say to you for a long time." She adjusted the collar of her raincoat, buying herself a moment of time. "I regret the way things ended between us. I still think divorce was the only answer for us, but I'm sorry you were hurt by it."

His eyes widened, as if he were stunned by the apology, then he gave a low, bitter laugh. "God, Anna, who are you trying to kid?"

"I'm serious," she said, a little wounded by his reaction. "I'm deeply sorry that I hurt you."

He took a quick step toward her and put a hand underneath her chin, tilting her face up to his. He wasn't a tall man, but he'd always worked out, always kept his physique lean and muscular. At five-six, Anna had never felt threatened or intimidated by his physical superiority, but now, gazing up at him, she saw something in his eyes she'd never seen before. The bitterness and the resentment were the same, the anger hadn't changed, but now there was another, darker emotion she couldn't quite name.

She wanted to move away from him, away from his touch, but something of the old Anna wouldn't let her cower away. She remained still, gazing up at him with what she hoped was a nonprovoking expression.

His gaze took on a mocking glint, as if he knew exactly what she was thinking. "Why, Anna," he said softly. "If I didn't know better, I might think they'd given you a soul along with that new heart. But the problem is…'' His features hardened almost imperceptibly. ''I do know you.''

He was still holding her face up to his, his dark eyes now burning into hers. Something smoldered in those black depths, something not quite sane, Anna feared.

Dear God, what had happened to him since their divorce? He'd been bitter and angry over the breakup, but she'd never considered him dangerous.

But now…the way he was looking at her…

Anna suddenly wondered if Hays was behind the phone calls. If he had a deeper, darker motive for his visit.

And she remembered just as suddenly the bouts of moodiness during their marriage. The bursts of temper. The way he would sometimes disappear for days at a time. He'd always blamed their marriage difficulties on her career, and Anna hadn't bothered to dispute him because she knew her ambition was a big part of their problem. But now she realized that their incompatibility went deeper than that. Much deeper.

''I once thought you were the most beautiful woman I'd ever laid eyes on. That blond hair.'' He tucked a strand behind her ear. ''Those dark eyes. And a body any man would kill to possess. But look at you now.'' His gaze roamed over her, taking in her pale complexion, her frail frame. ''Do you know what you've become, Anna? You're a freak, a modern-day Frankenstein.''

She tried to move away, but his grip tightened on her chin. ''It would be wrong to blame you, though, wouldn't it? The real monsters are the surgeons who patch together pathetic, soulless creatures like you from the dead and the dying.''

Anna said angrily, "Let go of me, Hays.''

His hand slipped to her chest, and with one finger, he uncannily traced the outline of her scar through her blouse. "Tell me something, Anna. What man is going to want to see that in bed?''

HAYS'S TAUNT followed Anna into her building, into the elevator, all the way up to the ninth floor. She'd experienced his animosity before, but nothing like this. He'd seemed so cold and cruel, and that strange glint in his eyes...

Anna shuddered, trying to put the confrontation out of her mind, but as she got off the elevator and walked down the hall to her apartment, she couldn't get his words out of her mind. *Tell me something, Anna. What man is going to want to see that in bed?*

It wasn't like she hadn't thought of that herself. It wasn't like she hadn't stared at that scar in the mirror, trying to picture a man's reaction the first time he saw it.

Luckily, she supposed, she had no one serious in her life these days. After her divorce, she'd avoided complicated entanglements and had pursued only the companionship of men who shared a similar philosophy to hers, namely, that she neither wanted nor expected an exclusive commitment, and her career would always come first.

She'd convinced herself it was an outlook that would serve her well, but looking back after her surgery, when she'd had plenty of time to dissect her life, Anna had come to realize that the like-minded men whose company she'd sought were as shallow as she, their personal lives as empty and vapid as hers. Looking at them was like looking in a mirror, and the reflection was not pretty.

Anna could well imagine their reactions on seeing her scar. Naturally, they'd try to put a good face on it, but inside they'd recoil in horror and wouldn't be able to get away fast enough. She was flawed now and—even worse—high-maintenance. A double whammy for the commitment-challenged.

And the one of substance, that nameless, faceless man whom Anna had now started to fantasize about? The man who could look at her, scar and all, and still want her? Was he out there somewhere?

Unaccountably, her thoughts went back to the man in the elevator, and as Anna inserted her key into the lock and opened the door, she wondered why he'd had such a strong impact on her. He was a total stranger. She'd probably never see him again. No reason for her to feel this strange fascination for him.

Except, of course, for the obvious reason. They were both flawed.

Had women shunned him because of his appearance?

Somehow Anna couldn't imagine that.

Closing the door behind her, she took off her soggy raincoat and tossed it into the powder room just off the foyer, an action that once would have been unthinkable to her.

"Laurel, I'm home!" She brushed fingers through her damp hair as she walked into the living room.

When there was no response, Anna decided she must have beat her stepmother home. Then she heard voices coming from the den, and she hurried down the hallway toward the sound.

"Laurel!"

As Anna entered the room, the first thing she saw was her stepmother's pale face, and she knew immediately something had happened. Something terrible.

Laurel stood in front of the television, so engrossed in whatever was on that she hadn't bothered to sit. She didn't appear to hear Anna's approach, either, but then she glanced up. "Anna! Oh, I'm so glad you're home. I've been so worried—"

She actually swayed on her feet, and Anna rushed to her side, clutching her arm. "Laurel, what is it? What's wrong?"

"I still can't believe it," she murmured, one hand to her throat.

"What?" Anna's gaze was drawn to the television screen then and to the news alert that had interrupted an afternoon talk show Laurel loved. A female reporter stood on the street in front of a large home in an older, upscale neighborhood.

But Anna caught only a word or two of the woman's report because her stepmother started to babble. "He must have left the hospital right after we did. The police think he was lured home and the killer was waiting for him—"

Anna gripped Laurel's shoulders. "What are you talking about? Waiting for whom?"

All Laurel could manage was to point weakly at the TV where the reporter's calm, clear tone was a surreal contradiction to her agitation.

Anna turned once again to stare at the screen. The reporter was in the middle of her recap. "…on the scene live in the Museum District where a prominent Houston heart surgeon was found brutally murdered in his home a short while ago. This has been a Channel Eleven exclusive report. Stay tuned for all the late-breaking developments…."

Anna spun to face Laurel. "No," she whispered.

Laurel nodded, her eyes brimming with tears. "It was Michael, Anna. He's dead."

And suddenly all Anna could think about was what her ex-husband had said to her not ten minutes earlier. *It would be wrong to blame you, though, wouldn't it? The real monsters are the surgeons who patch together pathetic, soulless creatures like you from the dead and the dying.*

HUDDLED INSIDE the apartment, Anna and Laurel remained glued to the TV that evening, watching several local news broadcasts for the latest developments in Michael's murder. But the details remained sketchy. He'd been shot to death in the breezeway between his garage and house. None of the neighbors had heard gunfire, nor had anyone seen anything suspicious. His body had been discovered when a woman walking her dog had gone to investigate her pet's frantic barking and strange behavior. No suspects were in custody, and though the police spokesperson didn't come right out and say so, it appeared there were no concrete leads.

After Anna went to bed that night, she lay awake for a long time thinking about everything Michael had done to save her life. And now *he* was dead. Who could have done such a thing?

Deep down, she didn't really believe Hays had anything to do with the murder, but his words continued to haunt her. When she finally fell into an exhausted sleep, however, she didn't dream about Michael or her ex-husband. She dreamed about the stranger with the scar.

He was lying naked in bed, watching her undress. His eyes were dark and smoldering, and as she slowly approached him, he reached up, snaking a hand around the back of her neck to draw her down for a long, deep, soul-shattering kiss that robbed her of breath and sanity.

For the longest time, they kissed. His tongue was deep inside her mouth, tangling with hers, mating with hers, making her yearn for an even deeper intimacy.

When they finally broke apart, she traced the scar on his face with her fingertip, and he let her for a moment. Then he grabbed her hand, pulling her on top of him, and she came willingly. Eagerly. She moved over him, and their bodies joined so frantically, she cried out. The stranger's hands slid downward, grazing her breasts, tracing her waist, grasping her hips as he set a powerful rhythm. Anna's head fell back. She could feel herself losing control. In another moment…

She woke up, gasping for breath. Her skin was on fire. For a moment, she thought it was the aftermath of the dream, but then she realized her elevated temperature and heart palpitations signified something far more dangerous.

Her body was rejecting her new heart….

Chapter Three

Anna climbed out of her car in San Miguel and stood in the baking heat. July in South Texas could be brutal and she was only a week out of the hospital. She'd rushed this trip. She knew that. She should have given herself another few days to build up her strength, but it was too late to turn back now. Somehow she knew if she got back in her car and drove away she might never work up enough courage to come here again. And if she left now, her self-doubts might never be laid to rest.

Everything about Anna's surgery and transplant had been almost textbook perfect. Michael had been so pleased by how readily her body had accepted the new organ and how quickly overall she'd recovered. Except for taking her daily meds, Anna had started to believe she could have a normal life again.

But Michael's murder and the organ rejection, coming on the same day, had been two devastating setbacks that had shaken Anna to her core. Both had been grim reminders of how fragile her world had become. Nothing was ever going to be normal for her again, and for the first time since the transplant, she'd begun to question whether or not it had been worth it.

Then, on the same day she came home from the hospital, she received a call from Tom Bellows. He'd discovered the identity of her donor. Her name was Katherine Sprague, a thirty-nine-year-old author and teacher who'd died of a gunshot wound to the head, leaving behind a daughter, a husband and a sister, all of whom still lived in San Miguel, a small town about thirty miles south of San Antonio.

But even more distressing than hearing about the family Katherine Sprague had left behind was the news of how she'd died. She'd put a gun to her head and pulled the trigger. Anna was alive because of another woman's utter despair.

Over the next few days, Katherine Sprague's suicide continued to haunt Anna. For hours on end, she pored over the notes Tom had faxed her regarding his investigation. She ordered all of Katherine Sprague's novels and read each of them in one sitting. She scoured the Internet for every scrap of information she could find. The research gave her something to focus on other than her own health problems and Michael's death. It gave her a purpose, a mission. It gave her a mountain.

But Anna also knew that her natural curiosity and interest in her donor's life was quickly becoming an obsession. She couldn't put Katherine's death to rest no matter how hard she tried.

And so she'd decided to come to San Miguel. Not to confront Katherine's family with the reality of her transplant, but to, in some subtle way, touch Katherine's life the way she'd touched Anna's.

She shivered despite the intense heat. She'd never particularly believed in destiny or fate, but she couldn't deny the connection she felt to the dead woman, or the strange pull she experienced as she stared up at Katherine Sprague's sprawling Romanesque-style mansion with its arched windows and towering palm trees.

Located on the edge of town, the house was perched atop a small hill that provided a sweeping view of the San Miguel River. The spacious grounds were lush and colorful, but even with the exotic ambience—or maybe because of it—the mansion had a brooding quality, a faint air of isolation even though the nearest neighbor was just down the street.

There was something about that house...

Anna could almost feel the whisper of its secrets along her backbone.

Before she lost her nerve, she hurried up the paved walkway, climbed the steps to the wide stone veranda, and rang the front doorbell. Perspiration dampened her blouse as she waited for her first encounter with Katherine's family.

A man answered the door. He was tall and well built, with broad shoulders, dark hair and piercing gray eyes that seemed to gaze at Anna with more than a fair amount of suspicion.

But the impression might simply have been her own conscience, she decided, trying to calm her nerves.

He was dressed in dark clothing that provided very

little contrast to the deep shadows in the hallway behind him. For a moment, he appeared little more than a shadow himself.

Except for those eyes...

Anna's breath quickened, and she experienced an odd sense of déjà vu as she gazed up at him.

Then the moment was over as he inquired impatiently, "Yes?"

Anna cleared her throat. "I'm—my name is Anna Sebastian. I'm here to see Gwen Draven. I believe she's expecting me."

"She lives in one of the guest cottages around back, but she's not there." His tone was blunt, still impatient. Not the least bit inviting. "She said something about running an errand. I guess she forgot she had an appointment." His gaze swept over her, and Anna winced inwardly at what he must see. A woman who, at thirty-four, should have been in the prime of her life, but instead was too thin, too pale, too fragile-looking to be considered attractive.

She'd pulled her blond hair back in the same French twist she'd worn for ages, a style that had once made her look cool and sophisticated, she'd been told. Now the severe fashion only highlighted her gauntness. Her eyes were shadowed underneath, and some of the medications made her hands tremble. At least, she tried to convince herself that was the reason for her sudden nervousness.

The man's gaze moved back up to her face. There was something in his eyes, an emotion she couldn't quite define, that spiked Anna's adrenaline to a dangerous level, leaving her a little light-headed.

She put a hand on the doorframe for support.

"Are you all right?" he asked with a scowl. "You don't look well."

"It's the heat—" She broke off as he shifted his position in the doorway, and a shaft of light fell across his face. For the first time Anna saw the scar, and her adrenaline surged once again, causing her heart to pound uncomfortably.

She knew him! He was the man from the elevator, the one who had captured her attention that day in the Chase Tower. The man she'd dreamed about so intimately...

Oh, my God!

Anna tried not to stare, but she couldn't help herself. Finding him here, in Katherine Sprague's house, jolted her.

"Maybe you'd better come inside and wait for Gwen." His tone had warmed slightly even though Anna knew he'd been aware of her reaction. And he undoubtedly thought it was because of his appearance.

"I—I don't want to impose." Anna was stunned to find herself stammering. She couldn't remember the last time she'd been so disconcerted.

"And I don't want you passing out on my doorstep." He stepped back and motioned her inside. "We can hear Gwen's car in the drive when she gets home. Come in," he insisted when Anna still hesitated. "I won't bite." And then, as she moved past him, she could have sworn she heard him mutter, "Not before sundown anyway."

Anna waited in the dim, cool hallway as he closed

the door, and then she followed him into a large living area off to the right. The room was done in autumn tones of browns and greens with an occasional splash of red thrown in for contrast. Strange wooden masks lined the walls, adding to the exotic flavor of the décor, as did the dramatic touches of animal prints in plush throws and pillows. The furniture and floors were a gleaming mahogany, but the plastered walls, high-beamed ceilings, and filtered light from a row of shuttered French doors kept it just short of oppressive. Anna actually found it cool and restful after the blistering heat of outdoors.

"My name is Ben Porter." He motioned her toward a seat. "I'm Gwen's brother-in-law."

"How do you do?" Anna recognized his name from Tom's research. He was an ex-cop who'd married Katherine Sprague just a few months before she died.

Anna wanted to believe her reaction to the man had everything to do with the rather bizarre coincidence of finding him here, but even that day in the elevator, when he'd barely glanced in her direction, he'd sparked something inside her. She'd told herself the scar on his face had drawn her attention, aroused her curiosity, but she wondered suddenly if it was something more.

And this house.

It was dark and foreboding, with its heavy furniture and shuttered windows, and yet there was something enticing about it just the same. Some mysterious pull that made Anna want to explore all of its deep, dark secrets.

Her gaze flickered back to Ben Porter. She suspected he had his own secrets, and she couldn't help wondering what it would take to unmask them. A kiss?

Almost against her will, she lifted fingertips to lips that were unexpectedly tingling. She knew, suddenly, what it would feel like to be kissed by this man. She knew his touch, his scent....

He'd haunted her dreams. So how could he possibly be a stranger?

A deep awareness flooded through Anna, and she trembled. She had Katherine's heart. Did she also have some of her memories?

No, of course not! It wasn't possible. A heart was just an organ. Tissue and muscle. It couldn't retain memory. And yet...

Could it really be just a bizarre coincidence that she'd seen Ben Porter that day in the elevator, felt the impact of his presence, and now their paths had crossed yet again? Here, of all places...

His gaze turned quizzical. "Are you sure you're okay? Why don't you sit down and I'll get you something cold to drink?"

"No, please don't bother," Anna managed to say. "I've already put you to too much trouble as it is."

"By letting you come in out of the heat?" He shrugged. "That's not a problem."

"But I'm interrupting your afternoon. Maybe I should come back another time."

"No need for that. Gwen should be home soon." He gazed at her for a moment longer, and then turned toward the door. "Make yourself at home. I'll be right back."

Anna watched him disappear through the arched doorway, and then she turned, gazing around. An ornate bombé chest on the far side of the room held a ceramic vase of orchids and several antique picture frames. Anna walked over and studied the photographs, then reached out and picked up one. It was the same black-and-white shot of Katherine that had been used on the jacket cover of her books.

She'd been an extraordinarily beautiful woman. A statuesque brunette with wide, dark eyes and full, sensuous lips. A woman of passions...

As Anna studied the photograph, she gradually became aware of the faint tinkle of a piano from somewhere deep in the house. She lifted her head, listening, as the seemingly random notes melded into a melody.

Heart and Soul.

"We have fresh lemonade," Ben said from the doorway.

Whether it was his voice or the music that violently startled her, Anna couldn't say for sure. But she dropped the silver frame, and the glass shattered against the wood floor. She stared at it in horror. "Oh, God. I'm so sorry." She knelt quickly and began picking up the glass shards.

Ben set the drink aside and moved toward her. "Don't bother with that. I'll take care of it later."

"I'm sorry," she said again. "I didn't hear you come in."

"I didn't mean to frighten you." His deep voice held a genuine note of regret.

"That music." Anna's hands were still trembling as she gazed up at him. "Do you hear it?"

He listened for a moment. "That's my stepdaughter, Gabriella. She's warming up for her piano lesson." He knelt beside Anna and put his hand on her arm. "I'm serious. Don't worry about the glass. I'll clean it up later."

A thrill snaked up Anna's arm at his touch. Their gazes met, his eyes darkened, and her stomach fluttered with awareness.

She tore her gaze from his and glanced down at Katherine's picture, which lay faceup beneath the fragments of glass. The woman's expression seemed at once amused and accusing, and Anna noticed suddenly that a tiny drop of blood was smeared across her features. "Oh, no! I've ruined the picture."

Ben shrugged. "There're plenty more around the house. Katherine was never camera shy." He reached out and took Anna's hand in his. "You've cut yourself on the glass. Let me take a look."

He turned her hand over and studied the tiny sliver on her thumb. "It's just a scratch, but you're still bleeding. Come on. I'll get you a Band-Aid."

"No, I'm fine—" The risk of infection was a constant concern since her transplant, and at any other time, Anna might have freaked about the cut. But now she was too distracted by the scars on Ben Porter's right hand to worry about her own well-being. The scars were long and smooth and deep, like the one on his face. She gazed at them, feeling oddly stimulated by the sight.

He got up abruptly as if all too aware of her scrutiny. "Come on. The bathroom is this way."

He led her down the hallway to a spacious powder room furnished in pink, gold and ivory. The décor in here was less exotic and utterly feminine, and Ben seemed overpoweringly masculine against the plush surroundings.

While he opened a gilded mirrored door and collected a box of Band-Aids and a bottle of antiseptic, Anna studied the chiseled line of his profile, the way his dark hair fell across his forehead, giving just a hint of vulnerability to an otherwise dark and brooding face. Shifting her gaze slightly, she saw that he was watching her watch him in the mirror.

A frown flickered across his brow, and Anna knew at once he thought she'd been staring at his scar. She hadn't been. She hadn't even noticed it.

It was his eyes that held her attention. Those lips...

The nerve endings connected to her heart had been severed during surgery. Her reaction to extreme emotion would be different from now on, Michael had warned her. So how was it possible that her new heart could pound so hard at Ben Porter's mere presence?

He turned slowly to face her, his gaze deep, probing. "You seem familiar to me." He searched her features, lifting a hand as if to smooth back her hair, but he didn't touch her even though Anna wanted him to. More than anything. She suddenly ached for his touch. "Have we met before?" he asked in a puzzled voice.

She shook her head, unable to speak. Unable for a moment to even breathe. What was going on here? What was wrong with her? How could she react so strongly to a man she'd just met? How could she want him…when she knew nothing about him?

Something odd happened to her then. The bathroom disappeared, and Anna found herself gazing down into Ben's smoldering eyes as her hair fell in a curtain around her face. They were in bed, naked, the covers twisted from their lovemaking, their skin shimmering in the afterglow. And he wanted her again. She could see it in his eyes. The passion. The longing. The desperation…

As if lost in the same vision, Ben grabbed her shoulders and pulled her to him, then tangled his fingers in her hair as he lowered his mouth to hers.

But just before their lips touched, Anna gasped and sprang back.

He stared down at her in shock. "My God," he muttered. "I'm sorry. I don't know what came over me. It's just…" He ran a hand across his eyes, as if trying to clear away the vision. "I'm sorry," he said again. "You probably think I'm some kind of pervert, grabbing you like that. But I swear I'm harmless."

As harmless as a cobra, maybe.

A door slammed somewhere nearby, and he looked instantly relieved. "That must be Gwen. I'll go tell her you're here while you take care of that cut." He backed toward the door as if he couldn't get away from her fast enough, but he paused in the hallway, glancing at her anxiously. "Are you sure you're okay?"

She lifted her chin. "Yes, I'm fine." She listened to the house for a moment. "The music," she said softly. "It's stopped."

Ben listened, too, and then shrugged. "Thank God for small mercies." Then he turned on his heel and disappeared.

A YOUNG WOMAN stood arguing with Ben in the dim living room. When she saw Anna hovering in the doorway, however, her anger instantly disappeared and she smiled brilliantly. "You must be Anna. Ben was just telling me you were here. I'm Gwen. We spoke on the phone this morning."

The first thing that struck Anna about Gwen Draven was her resemblance to her sister. She was a younger version of Katherine Sprague, but without the smoldering eyes, without the full, pouting lips and the hidden passions that, even in Katherine's photographs, seemed to ooze from her every pore.

Gwen's beauty was more subtle. And more wholesome somehow. She was only an inch or two taller than Anna and almost as slender, but where Katherine had exuded a steamy sexuality, Gwen radiated vitality. The line of tanned skin between her light blue top and her black low-rider jeans rippled with toned muscle.

Her hair was dark, shoulder-length and choppy, and when she carelessly pushed it back, the glossy strands fell perfectly back into place. She seemed the very epitome of youth, health and beauty, and yet when she approached Anna to offer her hand, there was a glimmer of uncertainty in her hazel eyes.

"I apologize for being late," she said. "I completely forgot you were coming."

"No apology necessary. I've obviously come at a bad time." Anna's gaze shot to Ben's before she glanced quickly away. It was disturbing seeing him now, a stranger again, when only moments ago... "I'm sorry for the intrusion."

Gwen waved aside her protests. "Don't be silly. My sister's friends are always welcome here."

Ben had moved slightly away from them, but out of the corner of her eye, Anna saw him whirl, as if something had caught him by surprise.

"You knew Katherine?" His tone sounded startled. "I assumed you were Gwen's friend."

"Gwen and I spoke on the phone this morning, but we'd never met until now." Anna was suddenly experiencing an acute attack of conscience. She'd wanted to meet Katherine's family, wanted to tell them *without telling them* what Katherine had done for her. To that end, she'd devised a cover, informing Gwen earlier that she'd gone to the University of Texas with Katherine and had only recently heard about her death.

It was a plausible enough story, Anna supposed. Through her research, she'd discovered they'd both attended UT, and even though Katherine had been in graduate school when Anna was a freshman, it was certainly possible their paths might have crossed at some point. But credible or not, Anna was finding the sham harder to pull off than she'd imagined. She didn't like deceiving Katherine's family. They deserved better from her.

But it was too late to change her plans now. Anna couldn't just blurt out the truth. They didn't deserve that from her, either. After all, if they'd wanted any contact with her, they would have responded to her letter.

Ben's gaze was still on Anna, and her skin went hot and cold from the intensity of his stare. "I guess I jumped to conclusions when you said you were here to see Gwen," he muttered.

"She and Katherine went to UT together," Gwen explained. "Anna's been ill and only just recently heard about Katherine's death. She called this morning to see if she could stop by." She turned to Anna, lifting a perfectly shaped brow for verification. "Did I get it right?"

She asked the question as if she suspected the story might be a fabrication. Or maybe her suspicions were a figment of Anna's guilty conscience. She moistened her lips, all too aware of both Gwen and Ben's scrutiny. "Yes."

"Were you close?" The edge in his voice sent a chill up Anna's spine.

"I beg your pardon?"

"You and Katherine. Were you close friends?"

She took a moment to formulate her response. "No, I can't say that we were," she said carefully. "But she had a very definite impact on my life."

"How?" He was scowling now, obviously displeased, but Anna had no idea why. Because of what had almost happened between them in the bathroom?

"It's… difficult to explain."

He looked on the verge of challenging her for that

explanation, difficult or not, but Gwen said smoothly, "A lot of people have said that about my sister. She had a special way of touching people's lives. Our father used to say she was like the Pied Piper. Her devotees would follow her anywhere."

"Exactly how well did you know her?" Ben persisted.

"For God's sake, you sound as if you're trying to interrogate the poor woman," Gwen scolded. "Don't pay him any attention, Anna. Once a cop, always a cop." She took Anna's arm. "Why don't we sit down?"

She guided Anna to a sofa luxuriously upholstered in a deep green chenille. Tossing aside a leopard-print pillow, she drew her legs underneath her and turned to face Anna. Ben remained standing. He hovered near the windows where the filtered light cast him in an unnatural aura.

Anna watched him for a moment before tearing her gaze away. "I can't stay long. I just wanted to stop by for a few moments."

"You can't go yet," Gwen protested. "We never have company anymore. Sometimes I think I'll go out of mind from boredom around here. We used to have people in and out of the house all the time, especially in the summer, when Katherine had her retreats here. Nowadays…well, it's just not the same without her, is it, Ben?" There was the barest hint of mockery in her tone before she turned her attention back to Anna. "Anyway, you said on the phone you're an attorney in Houston?"

"Yes, that's right."

"Did you and Katherine keep in touch after college?"

Anna paused. "No, not really."

"Then you'd probably like to hear a little about her life." Gwen smiled. "She was a tenured professor at the University of St. Agnes in San Antonio and the author of nine novels. Her books weren't all that successful from a commercial standpoint, but they acquired a certain amount of critical acclaim, and over the years, she developed something of a cult following."

"I've read her books and enjoyed them very much." Anna was relieved that at last there was a ring of truth in her voice.

"Ben is a writer, too, you know. That's how he and my sister met."

He turned from the window with an impatient gesture. "I'm not a writer."

"Yes, well, the only bestseller in this house has your name on it." Was that a touch of resentment in Gwen's voice?

Ben frowned. "That doesn't make me a writer."

"No," Gwen agreed. "But it made you a lot of money, didn't it? Not that you need it now," she added under her breath. She glanced back at Anna. "He and Katherine met at one of Ben's signings in Houston. It was at a little bookstore on South Main. Maybe you know it."

"No need to bore her with the details," Ben said dryly.

"Oh, don't be silly. What woman doesn't enjoy hearing a good love story? Especially one that in-

volves love at first sight.'' She gave Anna a sly smile.
''Katherine used to go on and on about how their eyes
met across the crowded bookstore…and then later,
how they couldn't keep their hands off each other. It
was a real fairy-tale romance. My sister was a very
lucky woman, Anna.''

So lucky she'd felt compelled to take her own life,
Anna thought.

Ben's mouth tightened as he glared at Gwen. ''For
God's sake, do you have to do this in front of a
stranger?''

Anna rose. ''Perhaps I should go—''

Gwen grabbed her arm and pulled her back down
on the sofa. ''No, please. Don't go yet. If Ben doesn't
want to talk about Katherine, we can change the subject. Perhaps he could tell you about his book. Now
there's an interesting topic.'' Her eyes gleamed with
something Anna couldn't define and wasn't sure she
wanted to.

She said cautiously, ''What's it about?''

''It doesn't matter,'' Ben said with a dismissive
shrug.

''It's about a serial killer.'' Gwen gave him a smug
smile, as if she enjoyed goading him. Anna had to
wonder about their relationship. The two of them obviously didn't get along, so why did they remain in
such close proximity to one another? Why hadn't Ben
moved back to Houston after Katherine's death?
What kept him in San Miguel?

''You're from Houston so you probably remember
all those murders three summers ago that the police

attributed to a killer they called Scorpio,'' Gwen was saying.

Anna forced her attention back to the conversation. ''Yes. As a matter of fact, a girl who worked in my building was one of the victims.''

Ben turned. ''What was her name?'' he asked sharply.

His tone took her by surprise. ''I don't remember. Renee something.''

''Renee Canard.'' It wasn't a question.

Anna nodded. ''Yes, I think that was it. She was killed in a parking garage across the street from my office. I didn't know her, but the police came and interviewed people in the building after her body was found.''

Gwen had been sitting quietly during this exchange, but now she said suddenly, ''What a strange coincidence. Ben was probably one of the cops you saw that day. You two may have even spoken, and now here you are.''

Anna's gaze went reluctantly back to Ben. She wondered if he was thinking the same thing as she, that maybe such a meeting, no matter how brief, was the reason they had this strange connection.

''The killer was never caught,'' Gwen said. ''Isn't that right, Ben?''

He started toward the doorway, as if he'd had enough of the conversation. ''If you'll excuse me, I have work to do.''

Gwen watched him leave, then turned back to Anna with a frown. ''You'll have to forgive Ben's manners. He's a little…abrupt at times.''

He'd left the room, but Anna could still feel his presence. It was so odd. She'd never felt this way before. She'd never experienced such an intense attraction, and she knew he'd felt it, too. Why else had he tried to kiss her?

She strove to keep her tone even as she said, "Is he working on a new book?"

Gwen grimaced. "No. He's working on an old case."

"He's still a cop, then?" Anna asked in surprise.

Gwen shook her head. "He's not a cop. Ben will never be a cop again. Scorpio took care of that."

"What do you mean?"

Gwen hesitated. "I don't know how much you remember about that summer, but the police had no real suspects. They were very frustrated. Ben was one of the lead detectives on the case, and he...did something stupid. He used himself as bait to draw out the killer, and he very nearly became Scorpio's thirteenth victim."

Icy fingers played up and down Anna's spine as Gwen leaned toward her, lowering her voice. "The scars on his hand and face...Scorpio did that to him. And the scars on the inside are even worse. I don't think Ben ever recovered from that summer. He's still convinced Scorpio will jump out of the bushes one day and finish him off."

Anna suppressed a deep shudder. Whatever Ben was afraid of, she doubted it had anything to do with his personal safety. He didn't seem the type of man to dwell on a close call, even one with a brutal killer. It had to be something else he feared. "I don't remember hearing about any more victims after that summer,'' she said reluctantly. ''The killings stopped, didn't they? The police thought Scorpio might be in prison for some other crime or else he was dead.''

Gwen shrugged. ''No one knows what happened to Scorpio, or why the killings stopped so suddenly. But all those unanswered questions still feed Ben's obsession.''

''Is that why he wrote the book?''

''Partly, I suppose. And partly because he was offered a great deal of money to do so. But enough of all this.'' She gave Anna an enigmatic smile. ''You didn't come here to talk about serial killers, did you? You came here to talk about my sister.''

''Actually, I just wanted to stop by for a few minutes to pay my respects and now I really should be going.'' Anna stood, suddenly anxious to get out of that house, away from Gwen Draven and her dark story, away from Ben Porter and his devastating effect on her. She needed space to breathe because for a moment while listening to Gwen, Anna had the disturbing notion that she was being sucked into Katherine's life and it just might be a place she didn't want to go.

To her relief, Gwen didn't protest her leaving. She got up to walk her to the door. ''Are you going back to Houston tonight?''

''No, I don't think so. It's a long drive, and I'm pretty tired. I think I'll find a place to spend the night, and then head back first thing in the morning.''

Gwen's gaze rested on Anna. ''Look, this is none of my business, but you mentioned on the phone this morning that you'd been ill recently. That's why you hadn't heard about Katherine.'' She paused. ''Are you okay now? You seem so...fragile.''

''I sometimes tire easily, but I'm fine,'' Anna evaded. ''Thanks for asking. And thank you for agreeing to see me today. It meant a lot.''

''I could tell that it did when you called.''

''Katherine changed my life,'' Anna said. ''I wanted her family to know that.''

Gwen smiled. ''Someday you'll have to tell me more about your relationship with my sister, but right now, I won't keep you. There's an inn on Old River Road called Casa del Gatos. It's sort of a cross between a bed and breakfast and a small hotel. It's actually quite charming if you don't mind rustic. When you leave here, just follow the street to the bottom of the hill and turn left. The hotel is all the way at the end. Some of the rooms have a nice view of the river.''

Anna nodded. ''Thanks. I'll look for it.''

The two women said their goodbyes, and Anna headed down the steps of the veranda, then crossed the lush grounds to the street. She paused at her car, glancing back at the house and wondering if she'd accomplished what she'd set out to.

Neither Gwen nor Ben had spoken about Katherine's suicide, but Anna supposed that was to be expected. She was a stranger after all. No reason they would open up to her.

But at least she'd been able to see for herself where Katherine had lived. She'd met her sister and husband, and had seen evidence of the very rich and full life Katherine had led.

So why had she committed suicide?

And why had Anna come away from Katherine's home deeply disturbed? It was as if there'd been something simmering just beneath the surface she hadn't quite been able to see.

As Anna stared up at the house, a movement from a third-story balcony drew her attention. Someone stood just beyond the railing, staring down at her. At first, she thought it was Gwen, but Anna wasn't sure even Gwen, for all her obvious physical fitness, would have had time to rush up two flights of stairs to the third story.

It suddenly occurred to Anna that the watcher might be Katherine's fourteen-year-old daughter, Gabriella, the one who had been playing the piano earlier. Anna couldn't distinguish her features, but for some reason she had the impression the girl was scowling at her with displeasure.

As their gazes met from a distance, a chill lifted the hair at the back of Anna's neck, and rather than waving a greeting, she opened the car door and climbed inside.

Chapter Four

Ben stood at the window of his second-floor office and stared down at the heavily landscaped grounds that were already deep in shadow even though the sun still lingered just above the horizon. Soon it would be twilight, and every bush and tree would become a potential hiding place for evil.

He grimaced, thinking that he might be starting to sound a little too much like Margarete Cortina, a local woman whose rants about demons and spirits, along with her devotion to a rather bizarre religion, had made her something of a laughingstock in San Miguel.

But Ben wasn't laughing, nor was he so quick to dismiss her beliefs as the ramblings of a mad woman. And for one simple reason. Like Margarete, he knew evil existed. He'd seen it. He'd almost been destroyed by it. And he would be a fool to dismiss the clues, no matter how subtle, that warned him now the evil was back. In a different form, maybe, but still deadly, nonetheless.

He flexed his right hand as he kept his uneasy vigil at the window. In the nearly three years since he'd been wounded, he still couldn't get used to the stiffness in his fingers, the loss of agility that made it impossible for him to fire a weapon with any accuracy. He still couldn't get used to the feeling of vulnerability that came with having hung up his .38 after fourteen years on the police force.

If Scorpio was back, in any form, Ben would now be easy prey.

But then, he always had been. He just hadn't realized it until it was too late.

A mistake he wouldn't make again.

His gaze fell on Anna Sebastian as she stood beside her car, gazing up at the house, and a dark foreboding stole over him. He'd never put much stock in premonitions or visions, but he still had a cop's instinct. Anna Sebastian was hiding something, and given her relationship to Katherine, Ben didn't think much good could come of her visit today.

Why *had* she come? What did she want?

Merely to pay her respects, as she claimed? Then why wait so long? Katherine had been dead for nearly a year.

He remembered Gwen mentioning something about Anna having been sick, and Ben could believe that. She was a pale, fragile-looking woman who seemed incapable of sustaining her own meager weight, much less holding up under the brutal South Texas heat. And yet in the short time he'd been in her company, Ben had sensed an inner strength. He'd glimpsed a steely determination in her eyes that her illness hadn't completely extinguished.

She was an interesting woman. Intriguing. And that

brought him back to his original question. Why was she here?

Maybe the better question was why had he reacted so strongly to her? For a moment in the bathroom, he'd forgotten they were strangers, and he'd completely lost himself in her sensuality, in those beautiful, soulful eyes that were so striking against her fair complexion. He'd almost kissed her, and not gently, either, but with a deep, driving need that had burned as hot as it was quick. He hadn't felt an instant attraction that fierce since...

He frowned, not wanting to judge her against his late wife, and yet knowing the comparison was inevitable. They were both beautiful women. Both secretive and coy. Both possessing that unique feminine power that could destroy a man's soul, if he wasn't careful.

Abruptly, Ben turned away from the window as Anna got into her car and drove off. Hopefully, that was the last he would ever see of her. He had enough to worry about without having to battle his own libido.

And yet even now he found himself wondering when she was leaving town. If he could arrange an accidental meeting...

Idiot, he scoffed. He'd never known when to leave well enough alone. That was why he was no longer a cop, and why he spent half his nights tossing and turning and the other half searching the darkness for ghosts.

Returning to his desk, he sat down and began to methodically go through his files. Since he'd left the police force, Ben had taken up the rather macabre hobby of keeping a body count of violent crime victims in and around Houston. He scoured newspaper accounts, badgered his contacts in the department, even kept in touch with some of the former detectives he'd worked with on Operation Exterminate, a task force assembled by the Violent Crimes Division to track Scorpio before the killer had suddenly gone dormant at the end of that summer.

This latest killing was the first one in nearly three years that had triggered Ben's deepest fears. Dr. Michael English's murderer had shot him in the head and then attempted to cut out his heart with a knife. A grisly little tidbit the police had withheld from the public.

Ben had been in Houston when he'd gotten word of the murder. His contact in H.P.D. hadn't known at the time if any of Scorpio's other signatures had been found at the crime scene, but at least he'd been able to warn Ben about the mutilation.

Most serial killers had their own unique calling cards that they left on the body or at the crime scene. In addition to removing the victims' hearts, Scorpio had stuffed dead scorpions in the victims' mouths. The absence of the latter in the English case didn't ease Ben's fear because he now knew—had known for almost three years—that Scorpio wasn't one killer but two.

The early consensus among the nearly three dozen detectives assigned to Operation Exterminate, as well as the FBI profiler who'd been called in to assist on the case, was that Scorpio, like most serial killers, was a male Caucasian. Ben's had been the lone voice of dissent, but even he hadn't realized until much later how truly unique Scorpio was.

As the media point man, Ben not only became the face associated with the investigation that summer, but also the cop Scorpio loved to taunt in the letters sent to the police station and to the newspapers, much as David Berkowitz had done in New York and the Zodiac had done in the San Francisco Bay area.

The writing appeared to be long, psychotic ramblings at first, but as the killings escalated, Scorpio's letters, especially the ones addressed to Ben, took on a more personal note, almost bordering on flirtatious at times. The killer began making references to the way Ben had looked on the news the previous evening, the color of his eyes, whether or not he'd just gotten a haircut.

The profiler picked up on the subtle coquetry, too, and suggested Ben use it to try and draw out the killer. He still wasn't as convinced as Ben, however, that Scorpio was a woman. Female serial killers were an anomaly and usually fell into two major categories: black widows and angels of death. Scorpio was neither. Scorpio seemed to be a true thrill killer, for which the act of taking a life was part of a desire for new and exciting kicks.

By the end of the summer, the game of cat and mouse had turned into a dangerous one of seduction. Whenever Ben was interviewed on TV, he made sure he gazed directly into the camera, as if he were speaking only to the killer, and he always wore a red tie, Scorpio's favorite color. The letters started to come with more frequency, containing subtle hints that soon it would be time for Ben and Scorpio to meet.

The profiler warned that the investigation had entered a new and even more deranged phase, and it might be time for Ben to pull back and assume a low profile.

But by then it was too late. By then Ben had fallen victim to the same fatal flaw that had been the downfall throughout the ages of better cops than he. He'd let the thrill of the hunt cloud his judgment, make him careless, and when he'd awakened one night in his darkened apartment to find himself staring up into the eyes of the killer, he'd realized then what Scorpio had known all along.

He'd never been in control. He'd always been one step behind, and when he'd joined the killer's deadly game, it had been because Scorpio had lured him in— not the other way around.

It was later determined that a drug had been slipped in Ben's drink when he'd stopped by a local bar with some of the other detectives working the case before going home that night. That was how brazen and confident Scorpio had become. The killer walked into a cop bar, slipped a Mickey to the highest profile detective in the city, and then calmly exited, with no one being the wiser.

The dosage was expertly administered, too. Ben felt nothing more than a faint drowsiness until he got home where he collapsed on top of the bed, fully dressed, as he often did after putting in fifteen-hour days.

When he finally awakened, his hands and legs were

bound with cord and his mouth taped shut to prevent the screams that surely would have been heard throughout the apartment complex once Scorpio set to work.

The killer started with Ben's face. One slash of the knife and no more TV appearances.

His right hand came next. The killer sliced deep, severing tendons, making sure Ben would never again qualify at the shooting range.

Even in his agony, Ben tried to remain alert for as long as he could, tried to commit certain things to memory. The killer's height, weight. The color of the eyes behind the ski mask. The size of the gloved hands that didn't tremble, that didn't show a moment's hesitation or a hint of mercy.

Woman or man? Ben couldn't honestly say. The disguise was thorough, the killer's movements carefully devoid of gender-related qualities. If the killer was a man, he had a slight build. If a woman, she appeared to be agile and athletic.

It was odd, Ben remembered thinking, that after months of tracking Scorpio, trying to get inside this monster's head, he'd always assumed when the moment of confrontation came, he'd feel some sort of connection, some sort of obscene bond with the killer, but there was nothing. Nothing but pain and rage...

And then, just before he lost consciousness, he saw her. The real Scorpio. She was standing in the shadows, watching. He couldn't see her face, but he knew instinctively the voyeur was female.

He tried to lift a beseeching hand, but she melted

even deeper into the shadows. And mercifully darkness soon claimed Ben.

The profiler, and later the police psychologist who came to interview him in the hospital didn't put much stock in his claim that Scorpio was not one killer, but two. Serial killer partnerships were rare, and even rarer still would be a female in the dominant position. The woman usually assumed the "slave" role, staging the torture and murder under the direction of her male "master."

Ben began to have his own doubts about what he'd seen. His pain and fear might well have made him imagine a third person in the room that night.

But then two days into his hospital stay, he'd awakened one night, sensing her presence. She'd been there. In his room.

It was impossible, of course. A guard was posted at his door. No one could get in without being seen. He must have had a nightmare.

But deep down, he knew it was no nightmare. Scorpio had somehow gotten past the nurses and the guard without detection. That was how clever, how resourceful, how utterly fearless she was.

She never came back. It was as if the sole reason for her visit was to prove to Ben how easily she could get to him.

The killings stopped, too. The game was over. Scorpio had won.

But little had Ben known then that in the dark, seductive game he'd set in motion that summer, Scorpio had one final move....

CASA DEL GATOS was a charming, turn of the century, Spanish-style inn with gleaming stucco walls and a red tile roof baked to a soft terra cotta by the relentless Texas sun. The long, curving driveway was lined with a neatly clipped hibiscus hedge in full scarlet bloom, and at one end of a wide veranda, a Mexican flame vine scaled a trellis to the low-hanging roof.

A gardener pushing a wheelbarrow came around the corner of the hotel and paused to watch Anna get out of her car and head up the steps to the entrance. He was a small, wiry man with a thick mustache and a dark, glossy ponytail that hung almost to his waist. A red bandana protected his neck from the sun, and Anna could see what appeared to be a tiny silver cross dangling from one ear lobe.

"*Buenas tardes*," she murmured, a little disconcerted by his unwavering stare.

He nodded but didn't say anything as he rolled the wheelbarrow toward the drive. Anna stared after him for a moment, then turned and entered the hotel.

The soft whir of ceiling fans overhead and the cool saltillo tile floor beneath her sandals were a welcome respite to the outside heat. As Anna gazed around, she had the strangest feeling of having stepped back in time. Like the tile roof, the heavy antique furnishings, ornate wall sconces and tasseled drapery had a faded, yesteryear patina that was at once quaint and faintly unsettling, as if the world had decided to stop turning in this one tiny oasis.

A large room opened up to the right of the lobby, and through a wall of windows on the far side, Anna glimpsed the wide, green slope of the lawn and just beyond, the silver glimmer of the San Miguel River.

No one was around to help her so she stepped up to the desk and rang the bell. After a few moments, a woman came through an arched doorway behind the desk, her gaze meeting Anna's and then, in one sweeping glance, taking in her slim skirt, sleeveless top, and sandals. She made no effort to disguise her disapproval, although Anna's attire was far from revealing.

She thought at first the woman was elderly, but on closer inspection, decided she was probably no more than fifty-five or so, around the same age as Laurel. But the similarity ended there. Laurel prided herself on her youthful appearance, and was always decked out in chic ensembles from her favorite boutique on South Post Oak. And she visited an expensive Galleria hair salon at least once a month for a cut and color.

The woman behind the counter did nothing to play up her rather striking features. She was very slender, but the shapeless, long-sleeve dress she wore all but disguised her figure. Her once black hair had gone almost completely gray, and she'd pulled it back in a severe bun at her nape, a style that seemed to detract from rather than enhance her truly beautiful obsidian eyes, and the high cheekbones and prominent nose that hinted at a Mayan ancestry.

"May I help you?" Her tone and expression were completely devoid of warmth, and Anna wondered fleetingly if she might be better off to get back in her car and drive out to one of the motels she'd seen on the freeway.

But chain motels left her cold, and even though the woman behind the desk was less than welcoming, the hotel itself had peaked Anna's interest. It was just the sort of picturesque, out-of-the-way place she'd always wanted to stay in, but had never taken the time to seek out.

"I'd like a room for the night." Anna automatically reverted to the curt, businesslike tone she'd used in dealing with difficult clients. "Preferably something with a view of the river," she added.

"For just one night?" The woman spoke carefully, with the barest trace of an accent, leading Anna to believe that English wasn't her first language.

"Yes."

"A single?" She pulled an old-fashioned registration ledger from beneath the counter and slid it toward Anna.

"A single is fine." Anna, in turn, handed the woman a credit card which elicited yet another look of disapproval before she plucked it from Anna's fingers and processed it in a machine she kept hidden beneath the desk.

The transaction completed, she returned Anna's card. "If you'll give me your car keys, I'll have your vehicle moved to the back."

"I'll need to get my bag out of the trunk first."

"Amador can bring it up to your room a little later." The woman took a key from one of the cubbyholes on the back wall. "I've put you in Room 209.

It has a nice view of the river. Turn right at the top of the stairs. It's all the way at the end.''

"Thanks."

As she handed Anna the key, her gaze flickered over her once more. "Is this your first stay in San Miguel?"

"Yes, as a matter of fact, it is."

"You have business here?"

Was the woman merely curious, or was that suspicion Anna saw glinting in her eyes? "Actually, I came here to pay my respects to the family of someone who died last year. You may have known her. Katherine Sprague?"

A startled, almost frightened look flashed across the woman's face before the hostile mask settled back into place. "Enjoy your stay," she said crisply. "Checkout is at 11:00 a.m. sharp."

ANNA COUNTED THE DOORS along the narrow hallway. Three on each side, and assuming the left wing contained the same number, that would make only twelve guest rooms on the entire second level. The Casa del Gatos was indeed a small hotel, and in spite of her less than friendly welcome from the woman downstairs, Anna was charmed by the old world atmosphere.

She wanted to make the most of her short stay, but her pleasure was dimmed by the woman's attitude. Why had she been so suspicious? Was it merely a natural distrust of all strangers? And why had she reacted so curiously when Anna had mentioned Katherine Sprague?

Anna had no idea, but she was suddenly too tired to worry about it. She opened the door of her room, leaving it ajar for the man bringing up her bag.

Taking a few steps inside, she gazed around. The room was small and sparsely furnished with a dresser, nightstand and a narrow bed fitted with a plain white coverlet. The walls were a stark white plaster, the only adornment a heavy wooden crucifix that hung directly over the bed.

The wide plank flooring creaked as Anna crossed the room. French doors led out to a common balcony that ran the entire length of the hotel and overlooked the lush lawn and river. A stray breeze whispered through Spanish moss dripping like liquid silver from heavy, ancient live oaks.

Opening the doors, Anna stepped out, hoping the breeze would be cooled by the water, but the day was still hot and muggy. She lingered for a moment, her gaze moving along the banks of the river where, in the distance, the stones of some old structure glowed in rustic hues in the late afternoon sunlight.

She glimpsed something red through one of the arched openings in the ruins and lifted a hand to shade her eyes. Someone was walking along the loggia.

A girl came through one of the archways and paused for a moment, glancing up and down the river as if sensing someone's eyes on her. Then she turned to disappear in the deep shadows of the ruins, and when she came back out, Anna almost missed her because she was no longer dressed in red, but in some drab color that blended perfectly with her surroundings.

She moved quickly down a stone trail that traced along the river, and after a moment or two, vanished into a dense stand of trees.

Anna continued to watch for a moment, intrigued by the girl's rather furtive movements, and then she turned to go back inside. It would soon be time for her evening medications.

Closing the door against the heat, Anna walked over and sat down on the edge of the bed, removing all the medicine bottles from her purse and lining them up like toy soldiers on the nightstand.

Something rustled behind her, and she turned, expecting to find Amador with her bag. Instead, a tall young woman in her early twenties stood in the doorway, her blue gaze fastened unblinkingly on the parade of pill bottles across the nightstand.

She must think I'm a junkie, Anna thought in amusement. She got up from the bed. "Yes?"

The young woman's gaze, startled and repentant, shot to Anna's. "I'm sorry." She wiped a nervous hand down the side of her jeans. "I was just about to knock."

"May I help you?" Anna asked coolly.

Struggling to regain her shattered poise, the woman smiled in a self-deprecating manner that was completely disarming. "I really wasn't trying to spy on you," she said ruefully. "Margarete asked me to tell you that dinner is served in the dining room between 7:00 and 10:00 p.m."

"Margarete?"

"She owns the hotel. She and her daughter, Acacia."

Margarete must have been the woman behind the desk, Anna decided. In which case, the woman's no-nonsense attitude, not to mention her obvious disapproval, didn't bode well for the room service Anna had been hoping for.

"Do you work here?" she asked the young woman.

"Oh, no." She gestured over her shoulder. "My room is just across the hall. I'm Emily Winsome."

A more fitting name, Anna couldn't imagine. The young woman was slender and delicate-looking with short, flippy blond hair and wide, cornflower eyes.

"I'm Anna Sebastian."

Emily smiled. "Welcome to the house of cats, Anna, although you're not likely to spot one around here these days. It's good to finally have someone else in the hotel. I was starting to get a little creeped out having this place all to myself."

Anna lifted a brow in surprise. "We're not the only guests here surely?"

"Unless you count Dwight Gump, but he's in and out a lot. Mostly out. He's a land man or something so he travels constantly. His room is in the other wing." She paused and smiled. "Don't let the silence freak you out too much. Things usually pick up on the weekends. There's an antique mall in town and a new water park out by the interstate if you like that sort of thing." She paused again, as if running out of steam, and Anna decided it was a good idea to let the conversation die a natural death. She was desperately tired, and a nap before dinner was almost a necessity.

Luckily, the man bringing her bag spared her from

an awkward dismissal. He was the same man Anna had seen earlier with the wheelbarrow, and when Emily saw him, she nodded and spoke, then turned back to Anna. "I'll leave you to get settled. Maybe I'll see you at dinner."

"Maybe." Anna smiled, but didn't commit herself. Instead she busied herself fishing money out of her purse.

"*Gracias,*" the man muttered, tucking the bills into his pocket. The silver cross hanging from his ear sparkled as he moved his head.

"*De nada.*" Anna followed him to the door and closed and locked it behind him.

A cool shower would have been a refreshing precursor to her nap, but she didn't even have the energy for that. Instead, she stepped quickly out of her skirt and top, and then, in panties and bra, crawled between the cool, cotton sheets.

Within minutes, Anna was dead to the world.

Chapter Five

Darkness swallowed the last of the light, and the shadows in the yard deepened. Luckily, the house was at the top of a hill, and from the veranda, Ben could see approaching cars for at least half a mile, but the night would hide anyone on foot.

An uneasy shiver snaked up his spine. He'd kept an almost constant vigil since he'd learned of the circumstances surrounding Dr. Michael English's murder, but he couldn't be everywhere at once. He couldn't watch the road and the river and the woods in back of the house. He couldn't catch a killer when that killer might be nothing more than a ghost.

But Ben didn't think that was the case. Even if Scorpio was dead, her partner could still be alive and on the hunt.

He had a theory about that. The woman he'd glimpsed in the shadows of his apartment that night— the real Scorpio, as he'd come to think of her—had derived her pleasure from *watching* the kill. She couldn't or wouldn't perform the act herself, might even have considered herself above it, so she had to seek out someone willing to do the wet work. Someone whose bloodlust equaled or exceeded her own, but for very different reasons. A missionary or visionary type killer, perhaps. One who followed the commands of some dark, inner voice....

Ben had been spared because he was a part of the game. Once the game was over...

A slight noise sounded from the end of the veranda, and Ben spun, almost expecting to find that his nemesis had managed to sneak up on him again. He let out a breath of relief when he spotted his stepdaughter hiding in the shadows.

"Gabby? Is that you?"

"Why do you always call me that?" she demanded, moving toward him. "You know Mother hated it."

"But you never seemed to mind it. In fact, I thought you liked it."

She shrugged, lifting a hand to shove back a hank of stringy dark hair. "Did you ever notice that Gabriella sounds a lot like Cinderella?"

"Hmm." Ben took a moment to consider her question. "Now that you mention it, I guess it does at that. But instead of two wicked stepsisters, you have just one clueless stepfather."

"You aren't clueless. Not completely, anyway," she allowed.

He sighed. "I am when it comes to kids, I'm afraid."

"But I'm not really a kid. I'm fourteen now."

"Yes, and I know even less about teenagers." Ben had grown up with two younger sisters, but Paige and Taylor had been nothing like Gabby. When they hadn't been on the phone gossiping and giggling about boys with their friends, they'd been in their rooms sulking about one thing or another. To Gabby's credit, she rarely sulked, but Ben had never heard her giggle, either. In fact, he'd hardly seen her smile, and he couldn't remember a time when she'd had friends over.

She spent most of her time on the computer, which worried him a great deal. But when he'd tried to counsel her on the dangers of online predators, she'd scoffed at his concern. "Do you really think I'm that dumb? I know better than to use my real name or give out my address. Besides, I can spot the real sickos a mile off."

And that assurance had made him feel so much better, Ben thought dryly.

He studied her now as she came out of the shadows, a tall gangly girl with a plain face and awkward mannerisms. Even in the darkness, he could see that she was dressed in her trademark drab beige, and he wondered again why Gwen didn't take the girl under her wing and try to get her out of those dowdy clothes and into something more age appropriate. Gwen wasn't exactly the clotheshorse her sister had been, but she had a sense of style. She could help the girl out if she wanted to.

But the sad truth was that no one in the household had ever taken much notice of Gabby, least of all her mother. Ben's late wife had been a gorgeous, charming, completely self-absorbed hedonist who'd had no business anywhere near a child, much less raising one.

"Who was that woman who was here earlier?" Gabby asked suddenly.

"Didn't Gwen tell you? She was a friend of your mother's."

"What did she want?"

Ben shrugged. "She'd just heard about your mother's death and wanted to stop by to pay her respects."

"What's her name?"

"Anna Sebastian."

Gabby glanced up at him. "You don't think it's weird that she waited so long to come?"

Her question mirrored Ben's own uneasiness, but he shrugged again. "She said she'd been ill."

Gabby was silent for a moment. "Did you think she was pretty?"

Ben frowned. "Attractive, I guess."

"As beautiful as Mother?"

"No one is as beautiful as your mother was." That much he could say truthfully about his dead wife.

Gabby sighed. "I wonder why she waited so long."

"Does it really matter? She's gone now."

Gabby's gaze searched the darkness. "But she'll be back, Ben. We both know that."

Something in her voice raised the hair at the back of Ben's neck. He had the sudden, spine-tingling notion that his stepdaughter was no longer referring to Anna Sebastian, but to her mother.

ANNA DREAMED about Ben and Katherine. They were together in a candlelit room scented with jasmine and wild orchids. Anna was there, too, a reluctant voyeur to their wild passion. As she watched them embrace, candlelight dancing over their nude bodies, her breath quickened, her blood heated, and suddenly it was she in Ben's arms, she who was kissing him with a wanton abandon she never would have imagined possible.

He kissed her as no man had kissed her before, held her as if he would never let her go, and when they fell back against the tangled sheets, their bodies melding, straining, she didn't know where her soul ended and his began. They were one, in every sense of the word.

Then he drew back, staring down at her. When he saw her scar, something dark moved in his eyes, something Anna didn't want to name.

He vanished like vapor before her very eyes, and when she reached out to draw him back, her hands touched nothing but air....

She woke up, gasping for breath, aroused by the dream and vaguely disturbed by it.

Squeezing her eyes closed, Anna willed away the unwanted images. She didn't want to be attracted to Ben Porter, knew that she was asking for trouble by indulging in such fantasies. And yet no matter how hard she tried, she couldn't force the forbidden visions from her head. It was as if she and Ben had been lovers, somewhere, in some other time, and he was in her blood now and always would be.

Her pulse gradually settling back to normal, Anna stared at the ceiling. She had no idea what time it was, but she thought it must be very late. Her room had grown dim and shadowy while she slept, but as she turned her head to glance at the bedside clock, she saw that it was only a little before nine. She hadn't missed dinner after all, which was a good thing. She wasn't the least bit hungry, but she knew better than to miss a meal. Low blood sugar could wreak havoc on her strength.

Swinging her legs over the side of the bed, she sat on the edge for a moment, trying to summon enough energy to shower and dress. Gradually, she became aware of the distant tinkle of a piano. She thought it might be her imagination at first, or the remnant of a dream, but when she pushed herself off the bed and crossed the room to open the French doors, the sound grew louder, more distinct.

She recognized the melody at once. It was the same one that had been played to her over her phone late at night. The same one she'd heard in Katherine's house. The same one, she realized now, that had helped lure her to San Miguel.

Heart and Soul.

A dark premonition settled over her then, and she quickly stepped back inside and locked the door. Hurrying across the room, she checked the lock on the door to the hallway, as well. Satisfied that the room was secure, Anna leaned against the wall and closed her eyes briefly.

Whether the music was a coincidence or something more sinister, she didn't know. But suddenly coming to San Miguel didn't seem like such a great idea after all.

FIFTEEN MINUTES LATER, she walked into the dining room downstairs, surprised to find the tiny space crowded with people. With only two guests in the entire hotel, she'd expected the place to be empty, but the two dozen or so tables were all occupied. She started to turn away, resigned to locating another restaurant in town, when she saw Emily Winsome waving to her from a table near the windows. The younger woman smiled and motioned her over.

"I wasn't sure you were coming down for dinner," she said as Anna approached her table. She looked especially pretty tonight in a sleeveless sweater the exact color of her eyes.

She was young, not yet twenty-five, Anna was certain, but she spoke and acted much older. She possessed a rare combination of sophistication and innocence that added to her considerable charm.

Anna glanced around. "Where did all these people come from? I thought we were the only guests registered at the hotel?"

"We are, but a lot of people from town come here to eat." Emily glanced around, as well. "All the tables seem to be full. Why don't you join me?"

"Oh, I couldn't impose on your dinner," Anna said quickly.

"You wouldn't be imposing. I'd enjoy the company. Please," she insisted when Anna still hesitated. "I'm serious. I hate to eat alone."

"Well, in that case, I'd love to join you." Anna pulled out a chair and sat down.

Emily smiled. "You won't be sorry. Margarete may be a little—well, actually, a lot—on the eccentric side, but she's a fabulous cook. Well worth the small inconveniences you have to put up with when you stay here.''

''Such as?''

Emily gave a delicate shudder. ''Like creaking floorboards in the middle of the night. Doors opening and closing at all hours. Took some getting used to, but now I don't mind. I just tell myself that waking up in the middle of the night, half scared to death, is part of the charm of this place.''

''I'll try to keep that in mind,'' Anna murmured. ''But what's with the name? You were right. I haven't seen one cat since I've been here.''

Emily grimaced. ''That's another of Margarete's idiosyncrasies. From what I understand, there used to be half a dozen or more cats roaming the grounds, all descended from a huge calico belonging to the man who built this place in the early part of last century. A few years ago, Margarete joined a weird religious cult, and she got rid of all the cats because she thought they were inhabited by the souls of the dead.''

Got rid of them how? Anna thought with a shiver. ''What about her daughter? What's she like?''

''Acacia?'' Emily said the name with a faint note of disapproval. ''I don't know anything about her religious beliefs, except that she claims to be descended from the Mayans who built the pyramid at Chichén Itzá. So I guess you'd have to say she's a bit on the eccentric side, too, but she's really nothing like her mother. You'll see for yourself soon enough. She usually comes in around dinnertime to help out. Unless, of course, she's giving a piano lesson.''

Anna glanced up in surprise. "She gives lessons here at the hotel?"

"Sometimes. There's a music room at the back of the hotel in their private quarters. But the students who can afford them have private lessons in their homes."

Relief flooded through Anna. That must have been the source of the music she'd heard earlier. It had been nothing more diabolical than a piano lesson.

But, of course, that still didn't explain the phone calls she'd received in Houston....

"Anna?"

She glanced up to find Emily gazing at her in concern.

"Are you okay?"

"Yes, I'm fine. Why?"

Emily shrugged. "I don't know. You look a little pale. I thought you might not be feeling well."

Was she wondering about all those medicine bottles she'd seen earlier? Anna wondered. "I'm fine, really. I just need something to eat."

"Let's order then." Emily summoned one of the waitresses who brought Anna a glass of water and a menu. Before she could open it, however, Emily said, "Everything here is delicious, but I highly recommend the fish tacos. Margarete has a special sauce that is out of this world."

"Sounds good." They both gave their orders to the waitress, and once she'd disappeared, Anna said, "You must have been here for a while if you've gone through the entire menu."

"A couple of weeks or so. I'm in town doing some research."

"Oh, are you a writer?" Anna asked curiously.

A brief frown flickered across Emily's brow. "Why would you think that?"

Anna shrugged. "I met someone earlier who'd written a book. I guess it was still on my mind."

"As a matter of fact, I do write, but that's not the kind of research I'm doing." Emily toyed with her water glass. "Actually, I'm still in school. I'm a graduate student at UT." She paused. "What do you do, Anna?"

"I'm an attorney."

"Oh, really." For some reason, Anna's profession seemed to interest her a great deal. "Where do you practice?"

"I'm with a firm in Houston. Or I was. I've been on leave for the past few months, and I may not go back. But I won't bore you with the details."

Emily took a sip of her water, but her gaze remained on Anna. "So what brings you to San Miguel? Business or pleasure?"

Anna shrugged. "Neither, really."

"You're here because of Katherine Sprague, aren't you?"

Anna stared at her in shock. "How did you know that?"

"I was in the sitting room off the lobby earlier when you came in. I heard you talking to Margarete. I wasn't deliberately eavesdropping," she quickly explained. "But the hotel is always so quiet. Voices carry."

When Anna didn't respond, Emily added unexpectedly, "It might surprise you to know that I came to San Miguel because of Katherine, too."

"You knew her?"

She nodded. "I did my undergraduate work at the University of St. Agnes in San Antonio. Katherine was one of my professors. She was the most fascinating woman I ever met. I still can't believe she's gone." Her expression turned sorrowful. "Every year she'd pick one or two of her students to attend her retreat here in San Miguel. I was lucky enough to be chosen a few years ago, and it was the most exciting summer of my life."

Their food arrived then, and they made polite small talk as they ate. But when the meal was over and the table had been cleared, Emily seemed anxious to return to their previous discussion.

"So how well did you know Katherine?"

Anna gave her the stock response. "Not all that well. But she made a very big impact on my life."

"In what way?"

Anna hesitated. "It's a private matter. I don't feel comfortable discussing it."

"I understand, and believe me, I'm not trying to pry." Emily hesitated. "But it just occurred to me that you might be the perfect person to help me."

"Help you with what?"

An emotion Anna couldn't define flashed across the younger woman's features, making her look anything but winsome. Her mouth hardened, and the dark gleam in her eyes caused Anna to suddenly shiver.

She leaned across the table and lowered her voice. "Help me prove Katherine was murdered."

Chapter Six

Ben could tell something was still bothering Gabby, and he suspected it was more than Anna Sebastian's unexpected visit that afternoon. The anniversary of Katherine's death was coming up, and the memories of the day were bound to weigh heavily on the poor kid.

What she needed was a diversion, he decided. Maybe they both did. "Why don't we drive into town and rent a couple of videos? You get to pick. I'll even throw in some popcorn."

Gabby shrugged, disinterested. "I can't. I'm waiting for Acacia."

"At this hour?" He glanced at his watch. "It's after nine. That's a little late for a piano lesson, isn't it?"

Her shoulders lifted again. "She couldn't make it this afternoon so she called and asked if she could come over tonight."

"Why didn't you just postpone it until tomorrow? Or better yet, why not take a break from the lessons until school starts back? I'd like to see you have some fun this summer, Gabby. You don't need to be tied down to the same rigid schedule.''

She gave him a reproachful look. ''Mother wouldn't have liked that. You know what she used to say. I need all the practice I can get.''

That sounded like Katherine. She'd never cut Gabby any slack. In fact, at times, she seemed to enjoy twisting the knife in the kid, and that from a woman who could have afforded a little compassion, considering her own natural assets had been an embarrassment of riches.

Everything had come too easy for her. She'd been a novelist and teacher by profession, but she was equally gifted as a poet, artist and pianist. And she'd been gorgeous, the kind of woman who could make good men do very bad things.

Like marry her in the heat of the moment, Ben thought grimly.

The impetuous trip to Las Vegas just two weeks after he and Katherine had met in Houston wasn't exactly a testament to his own good sense, let alone his self-restraint. Waking up cold sober the next morning, he'd known immediately the marriage was a terrible mistake, but Katherine had ways of making him forget his bad judgment. At least temporarily.

After the initial attraction had worn away, they'd both realized there wasn't much left worth salvaging. When Ben had finally taken a long, hard look at the woman he'd married, he'd been astounded by the depth of her deception and by his own sheer stupidity.

He was a classic example of a man who hadn't been thinking with his brain or his heart, but with the part of his anatomy that had never been a very good judge of character. There had never been anything between him and Katherine except mind-blowing sex.

And, of course, the terrible suspicions he'd begun to harbor before she died.

He'd never thought of Katherine as the type of woman who'd commit suicide, but the selfishness of the act was just like her. After all, she wouldn't have wanted to wait for a debilitating disease to sap her energy or old age to ravage her looks. She would have wanted to pick the time and manner of her own demise, leaving behind questions, suspicions and those dark secrets that Ben feared now might never be revealed.

It was those secrets that kept him in San Miguel. Those secrets and Gabby. He couldn't leave her with Gwen. Not when his sister-in-law was starting to remind him more and more of Katherine.

And now with this latest murder...

"You know the real reason Acacia wants to come over tonight, don't you?" Gabby asked. "She's coming to see you."

"Oh, I doubt that." He punched Gabby's arm playfully. "In case you haven't noticed, I don't exactly look like Brad Pitt these days. Not that I ever did."

"You think those scars make you ugly, but they don't. Mother didn't think so, either. She always said they made you look mysterious. She loved them."

Ben flexed his right hand. Katherine had told him the same thing that first night they'd met, but he hadn't understood then that she really meant it. Or why. He thought she was being kind. What a joke.

He and Gabby watched silently as a car pulled into the driveway and the engine was shut off. After a moment, the lights went out, a door slammed and footsteps sounded on the stone stairs.

Acacia Cortina paused when she saw Ben and Gabby on the veranda, and her hand flew to her heart. "*Dios mío!* I wasn't expecting to see anyone out here." She gave a breathless laugh. "You startled me!"

She was in her late-twenties, slender, elegant and exotically attractive with long, black hair and wide-set brown eyes fringed with lashes heavily coated with mascara. Her red lipstick matched the tint on her nails and the sleek sundress that left very little to the imagination.

"Why aren't you doing your warm-up exercises?" she admonished Gabby. "Go on in, and I'll join you in a moment. I'd like to have a word with Benjamin. Privately," she added, when Gabby hesitated.

Gabby cast Ben an I-told-you-so look before she turned and disappeared inside the house.

Acacia laughed again as she adjusted one of the straps on her sundress. The action drew Ben's gaze to her impressive cleavage, which, he supposed, was the whole point.

Contrary to what he'd told Gabby, he'd been aware for sometime of Acacia Cortina's none too subtle come-ons, but he didn't delude himself into thinking she was interested in him because of his looks. He had an idea his bank account might have something to do with her attraction. Katherine's will had made him a wealthy man.

"I know what you must be thinking." She smiled provocatively. "A piano lesson at this time of night is a bit unusual. I had to help Mama at her church today, but I didn't want to cancel Gabby's lesson altogether."

"It wouldn't have been a problem if you had," Ben said with a shrug. "Missing one lesson isn't going to hurt her."

"I know what you mean." Acacia sighed wearily. "I've never tried to teach a child with such a tin ear."

That wasn't what Ben had meant at all. "Look, maybe what she really needs is a break from her routine. I'm thinking of canceling her lessons until the end of the summer."

Acacia glanced at him in alarm. "*No puedes!* Please don't do that!"

Her response took him by surprise. "Why not?"

She took a moment to collect herself. "Forgive me, Benjamin, but I don't think that would be a good idea. What Gabriella needs right now *is* her routine. She needs to know there are some things in her life she can always count on."

"I don't see how skipping a few piano lessons can do her any harm," Ben argued.

"But it isn't just the lessons," Acacia rushed to assure him. "I want her to know she can count on me, too. A teacher can have a powerful influence on a student. I like to think that I can make a positive difference in Gabriella's life."

She moved up beside him before he could object and placed her hand on his arm. "I think I can help you, too, Benjamin, if you'd allow me to."

"Look, Acacia—"

"Shush." She reached up and put a finger to his lips. "Katherine's been gone a long time. You're still a young man. You must have needs." She leaned toward him, parting her full red lips in invitation.

He cleared his throat. "I, uh, think you may have the wrong idea—"

She cut him off again. "No. I think *you* have the wrong idea about me. You can't imagine what goes on inside my head, Benjamin. The thoughts I have." She gave him a seductive smile. "I have needs, too, you know."

Someone laughed behind them, and Acacia spun. "Who's there?"

A set of French doors opened from the library onto the veranda, and Ben could see Gwen standing just inside.

Acacia saw her, too, and her features tightened in fury. "How dare you eavesdrop on a private conversation?"

"How dare you put the moves on a man whose wife is barely cold in her grave?"

Acacia gasped in outrage. "Katherine's been dead for almost a year!"

"Yes, and you must have waited a whole ten minutes after hearing the news before you made a beeline over here."

"That's not true!"

"It most certainly is."

Acacia stamped her high-heel sandal in outrage. "You haven't changed a bit since we were in high school. You were always *una canalla*. Evil.'' She spat the word as she made the sign of the cross.

''Oh, cut the dramatics,'' Gwen said in a bored tone. ''Sprinkling a few Spanish phrases into your vocabulary doesn't make you exotic any more than claiming to be a reincarnated Mayan princess makes you some kind of royalty.'' She turned to Ben. ''She's peddled that story for years, but everyone in town knows it's as phony as her mother's religion. But at least Margarete honestly believes she sees demons lurking behind every bush. Acacia's just out to catch herself a rich husband.''

''Una canalla,'' Acacia muttered darkly.

Gwen laughed which further infuriated the other woman. In another second, they'd likely be at each other's throats, which didn't particularly worry Ben, but he didn't care to be caught in the middle.

''Ladies, if you'll excuse me—''

''No, don't go!'' Acacia reached for his arm, curling her bloodred nails around his wrist. ''I'm sorry she had to misconstrue my offer of friendship.''

''Misconstrue, my ass,'' Gwen said bluntly.

''Perhaps we can talk later,'' Acacia murmured to Ben. ''Somewhere more private.'' Then tossing her hair, she flounced inside, leaving a cloud of some heavy perfume in her wake.

Gwen laughed again as she stepped out onto the veranda. ''Offer of friendship. That's a good one. A word to the wise, Ben, that little tramp's 'befriended' half the men in this county.''

''She used to be *your* friend,'' Ben reminded her. ''Don't you think you were a little hard on her?''

Gwen snorted. "Acacia Cortina and I were never friends. Whatever gave you that idea?"

"Katherine mentioned it once."

Gwen straightened her shoulders. She wore a white shirt tied at the waist and trim khaki slacks that made her look about the size of a pencil. She was in great shape, worked out obsessively, but there was something almost masculine about her toned body. "My sister was not the be-all and end-all authority on me. She was the one who used to let Acacia follow her around like some lost puppy. But that was Katherine. Always looking for new strays to worship and adore her." She cut Ben a sidelong glance. "Present company excluded, of course."

He said nothing as she came to stand beside him on the veranda. "What are you doing out here anyway? I've seen you out here every night for the past week or so, just staring off into the darkness."

He shrugged. "I like fresh air."

"Liar. You're looking for something. Or someone." Her smile turned cunning. "Did it never occur to you, *Benjamin*, that you just might be looking in the wrong place?"

She turned then and went back inside, and Ben was left alone once more. His gaze scanned the darkness, and when a shadow moved near the street, he froze. He stared at the spot for a long time, telling himself his imagination was playing tricks on him. No one was there.

But just when he almost had himself convinced, the moon slid from beneath a cloud, revealing the outline of a woman hovering at the edge of the yard.

She was standing very still, staring up at him, and as their gazes met in the darkness, Ben felt the blood in his veins turn to ice.

Turning, he raced down the steps.

ANNA STARTED VIOLENTLY as someone came up behind her, moving so silently she didn't hear his approach until he was on her. Before she even had time to scream, he grabbed her and spun her around to face him. Her frightened gaze shot to Ben Porter's furious scowl, and a sudden adrenaline rush caused her heart to jump erratically. Dangerously.

"What are you doing out here?" he growled.

He was still holding on to her shoulders. Anna winced and tried to move away, but his grasp only tightened. "Answer me! What are you doing out here?"

Anna tried not to let her nerves show. She lifted her chin defiantly. "I decided to take a walk after dinner. No law against that, is there?"

His gaze narrowed. "And you just happened to walk by here?"

She shrugged. "Yes, as a matter of fact. I'm staying at the Casa del Gatos. It's not that far from here." She tried to move away from him, but he held on to her. "Look, I'm sorry to have bothered you. I'll get on with my walk and you can go back to…whatever it was you were doing."

His grip on her eased, but he still didn't release her. "Do you always take walks after dark?"

"Sometimes, when I can't sleep. Walking is part of my physical therapy."

His gaze darted over, taking in again her frail appearance, and then he did release her. So abruptly Anna stumbled a little. He ran a hand through his dark hair. "Sorry I grabbed you like that. I hope I didn't hurt you."

"I'm not so frail that I'll break if someone touches me." Now why had she felt compelled to reassure him of that?

He studied her for a moment. "You really shouldn't be out walking alone after dark. You're from Houston. You should know better."

"We're not in Houston. And San Miguel seems like a safe place."

"Yeah, well, so did Paradise," he muttered. "And evil still found a way in."

A shiver slithered up Anna's spine. She knew instinctively that he was thinking about Scorpio, and she couldn't help remembering what Gwen had told her earlier. *He's still convinced Scorpio will jump out of the bushes one day and finish him off.*

Was that why he was so angry? Had he thought she was Scorpio? Surely he wasn't *that* paranoid.

But as Anna gazed up at him, taking in his dark, hooded eyes, his sensuous lips, she had a sudden insight into what he'd been through the past three years. Every time he looked in the mirror, saw that scar, he would think of the killer who had gotten away. A killer who might still be out there somewhere, preying on the innocent. Ben would take that personally. He wouldn't be able to rest until the killer was either dead or brought to justice.

Scorpio was Ben's obsession, just as Katherine Sprague had become hers.

"I'd better go," she said abruptly.

He reached out and put a hand on her arm. "Why did you really come back here? You didn't just happen to walk by here, did you?"

She hesitated. "I guess I wanted to see Katherine's house one last time. To say goodbye, in a way."

"Because she made a big impact on your life."

His grim tone made Anna shudder. "Yes."

His gaze deepened in the moonlight. "I wish you'd explain that."

"I...can't."

"Why not?"

Anna tucked a loose strand of hair behind her ear. She'd worn her hair down tonight, although she had no idea why. "Does it matter? I'm going back to Houston tomorrow. You'll never see me again."

Was that a look of regret that flashed in his eyes, or merely Anna's own wishful thinking?

His hand reached up and before she could stop him, he trailed his fingers through her hair. Not that she would have stopped him anyway. She seemed to have no power over her response to him, and that was a foreign concept to Anna. She'd always been the one in control—of her life, her career, her relationships. She was the one who backed off when things got too serious, when a liaison headed in a direction she didn't want to go.

She wasn't backing off now, and that frightened her. Ben Porter frightened her, and Anna knew if she were smart, she'd go straight to the hotel, pack her things and head back to Houston tonight. The best way to honor Katherine's memory was to get on with her new life, make the most of this second chance.

But the only action Anna seemed capable of at the moment was to gaze deeply into the eyes of Katherine's husband.

She thought about the way he'd almost kissed her earlier that afternoon, and she wanted him to again, but this time she wouldn't stop him. This time she'd succumb to the strange pull that had brought her back here tonight.

She hadn't come here to say goodbye to Katherine at all, she realized. She'd come here hoping to see Ben.

He suddenly avoided her gaze, as if sensing the direction of her thoughts. "I'll walk you back to the hotel."

"That really isn't necessary."

"It is for me."

She didn't argue further, and an uneasy silence fell between them as they started to walk. Rather than heading back the way Anna had come, Ben showed her a shortcut along the river. The earlier cloud cover had scattered, and moonlight glittered brilliantly on the water. Lights from houses perched along the banks twinkled on, and Anna could hear the occasional burst of laughter from boats anchored on the water.

They were far from being isolated, but Anna was nervous just the same. She was alone with Ben Porter, a man who was virtually a stranger to her, but she didn't fear for her life. She suddenly feared for her heart. She'd never believed in love at first sight, but how else to explain this sudden, powerful attraction?

Had it been this way between him and Katherine?

Katherine used to go on and on about how their eyes met across the crowded bookstore…and then later, how they couldn't keep their hands off each other. It was a real fairy-tale romance. My sister was a very lucky woman, Anna.

Anna frowned as she remembered Gwen's words. "Ben—" It was the first time she'd used his name, and the familiarity of it, the intimacy of it, shocked her.

He turned to glance down at her. "Yes?"

She hesitated, drawing a deep breath and then losing her nerve. "Nothing. It doesn't matter."

"You don't want to tell me what you were about to say?"

"It's none of my business."

"Why don't you let me be the judge of that?"

"All right, I will." A stray breeze from the water lifted a strand of her hair, and she carelessly pushed it back. "This afternoon when I came to your house, I sensed some tension between you and Gwen. Or was that just my imagination?"

He shrugged. "It wasn't your imagination. I'm not one of Gwen's favorite people."

"Why not?"

"She didn't approve of my marriage to her sister."

Anna glanced up in surprise.

"It's complicated," he said with another shrug. "Gwen and Katherine's parents died when Gwen was only eleven and Katherine was twenty-one. Katherine pretty much raised her, and I think Gwen came to think of her more as a mother than a sister. She resented anyone who took Katherine's time and attention away from her.''

''But what about Katherine's own daughter? Gabriella, you called her.''

He nodded. ''Gabby's fourteen. Gwen pretty much ignores her, but then, so did Katherine. The poor kid's had to raise herself.''

Well, at least he hadn't been blinded by his love for Katherine, Anna thought. He'd still been able to see and acknowledge her faults.

''Is Gabby the reason you've stayed on in San Miguel since Katherine's death?''

''She's part of the reason. She's had a hard enough time adjusting to her mother's death. I don't want to add to her pain.''

Anna paused. ''Have you thought about taking her back to Houston with you? Maybe a change of scenery would do her good.'' She winced as she said it, wondering if he could see right through her motivation. If he took Gabby back to Houston, then perhaps he and Anna…

Ridiculous thought. Dangerous thought. She had to put it out of her head. There was no her and Ben and never could be.

''Gwen seems okay with the situation as it is, but if I tried to take Gabby away from here, she might decide to fight me for custody.''

''But if Gwen just ignores her, why would she care?''

His voice hardened. ''Whether Gwen wants Gabby

or not isn't the issue. She's Katherine's daughter. If I tried to take her away from here, Gwen would have a problem with that."

"I'm not sure I understand that reasoning," Anna said.

He glanced away. "Like I said, it's complicated."

They walked on in silence for several more minutes. Anna looked up as a breeze drifted through the trees. The leaves rustling overhead sounded like rain, and the Spanish moss hanging from the live oaks rippled like ribbons of silk. The night was alive with the sound of crickets and bullfrogs and the distant hum of a motorboat.

Sometime during the past few moments, Anna had begun to relax in Ben's company. In fact, it was starting to seem perfectly natural for her to be walking along the river with him, asking him personal questions that he didn't hesitate to answer. She wondered if he found this development as surprising as she did.

She stopped for a moment, not because she grew winded from the walk, but because she suddenly wanted to prolong her time with him. Tomorrow she would leave for Houston and she might never see him again. The notion left her a little bereft, although she knew there was no rational reason for her to feel that way.

He paused, too, gazing down at her in the moonlight.

Anna could feel her senses—too long dormant—tingling to life. "You said Gabby was only part of the reason you've stayed on in San Miguel. What's the other reason?"

He frowned. "Let's just say, I have unfinished business here."

"Does that mean you plan to stay in San Miguel indefinitely?"

"Yeah, I guess it does."

She wondered if he understood her regretful sigh. "I'm leaving for Houston first thing in the morning. I guess that means this is goodbye."

"If this is goodbye," he murmured, "Then there's something I have to know before you go. Something I've been wondering about since the first moment I laid eyes on you."

Anna caught her breath at the look in his eyes. "What?"

He didn't answer her. Instead he cupped her face in his hands and lowered his mouth to hers.

Chapter Seven

What he was doing was crazy, and a split second before he kissed her, Ben half hoped she'd come to her senses and push him away. But she didn't. Instead, when he drew her to him, she came willingly, eagerly, tilting her head back invitingly as her eyes drifted closed.

He took another split second to stare down into her upturned face, telling himself that she wasn't his type. She was tiny and frail and looked too damn much as if she needed someone to take care of her. He didn't want the job. He had too much on his plate as it was.

And yet kissing Anna Sebastian was like breathing. He couldn't *not* kiss her. He had to. He had to taste her, touch her. Somehow he had to get her out of his system.

And so he let it happen.

He told himself he'd be gentle with her. He'd take it slow and easy, and if she pulled back, if she gave even the slightest resistance, it would be over. He'd chalk it all up to a moment of madness. He'd go home and forget all about Anna Sebastian.

But she didn't resist and he wasn't gentle. The moment his lips found hers, slow and easy went out the window. Her mouth opened beneath his, and his tongue plunged inside, just like that. He pulled her to him, and she melted against him, her body willing and pliant beneath his hands.

She looked so cool and untouchable on the outside, with her pale blond hair and those dark, fathomless eyes. But inside, a fiery passion pulsed through her veins. He could feel it in the heat of her skin, in the way she kissed him back, so fiercely Ben could hardly breathe, let alone think straight.

And she was a lot stronger than she looked, too. He could feel how toned she was through her clothing. Her body wasn't all hard angles and rippling muscle like Gwen's, but with enough feminine curves and softness to be all woman. No mistake about that.

No mistaking her intent, either, when she slipped her hands inside his shirt, touching skin he knew was as red-hot as her own.

He allowed her to explore for as long as she wanted, and then when her hands faltered at the waistline of his jeans, he took over, quickly unbuttoning her blouse to slide his hand inside, cupping one of her breasts through the lacy fabric of her bra.

She gasped and broke the kiss, letting her head fall against his shoulder. She didn't remove his hand, though. Instead, she lifted her own to cover his. "Oh, my God," she whispered raggedly. "What are we doing?"

"I can feel your heart beating," he murmured. "It's racing."

"It's not supposed to do that."

"What?" He kissed her hair.

His hand was still on her breast, and with his thumb, he drew a circle around her nipple. She gasped, but didn't lift her head from his shoulder. It was as if she didn't dare move for fear of losing the moment.

He widened the circle, then slid his hand across her chest to the other breast, pausing very briefly on the ridge in between. "You've got a scar," he said in surprise. "What happened?"

She jumped away from him as if he'd burned her. Hugging her blouse tightly around her, she turned her back to him as she quickly redid the buttons.

"I don't know how I let that happen," she said in horror. "I don't know what came over me."

"You mean what came over us both."

"I should have known better." When she turned back around, her blouse was completely done up. Lifting a shaky hand, she smoothed back her hair. "I've never done anything remotely that impulsive or irresponsible in my entire life."

Ben wished he could say the same. Now that the moment was over, he was having his own set of misgivings. If his marriage to Katherine had taught him anything, it was that giving into impulses usually led to nothing but regrets in the morning.

Besides, he couldn't afford to get involved with anyone right now because he couldn't afford to be distracted. He'd let down his guard once. Never again.

Anna had moved away from him and was staring at the river. After a moment, she lifted her hand to point across the water. "What's over there? It looks like the ruins of an old church. I saw it today from my hotel room.''

Ben followed her gaze. ''It's Mission San Miguel,'' he said with a frown. ''One of the last missions the Franciscans built in this area. It's not as famous as the San Antonio missions, or as well preserved, but it does have an interesting history.''

''I can see the bells,'' Anna murmured.

''Believe it or not, you can even hear them ring sometimes when the wind is up.''

''It's so beautiful in the moonlight it takes my breath away,'' she said.

He studied her as she studied the mission. *She* was beautiful in the moonlight. Her skin was pale and flawless, her hair a fine gold shimmering about her shoulders.

Her dark gaze lifted to his, and his blood heated in awareness.

''How do you get to it?'' she asked curiously.

''There's a bridge in town over the river. The road leads right by the mission.''

''What about from the other direction?'' She pointed downstream.

He shook his head. ''There's not another bridge for several miles. When the water is down, you can actually walk across in places. But we had an unusually wet spring, and this is the deepest and widest part of the river. The only way across around here is by the bridge in town or by boat.''

''That's strange,'' she said with a little frown. ''I saw someone over there today from my hotel room. When she left, she took off in that direction.''

"She?" The nerves in Ben's stomach knotted painfully.

Anna nodded. "I think it was a girl or a young woman. I couldn't really tell her age from such a distance, but I got the impression she was young. And I had the oddest feeling she didn't want to be seen. Her movements were…furtive somehow." She hesitated. "And another thing. When I first saw her, she had on red, but then she went inside the ruins, and when she came back out, she'd changed her clothes. She was wearing something dark and muted that blended with the stones. I almost missed her."

A fist closed over Ben's heart and squeezed so tightly he could hardly breathe. "Are you sure?"

She glanced at him in surprise. "Of course, I'm sure. Someone was over there—"

"No." He grabbed her shoulders almost fiercely. "I mean about the red. Are you sure she was wearing red?"

He'd frightened her. He could see it in her eyes, feel it in the way she tried to pull away from him. He hadn't meant to, but he couldn't seem to help himself. What she'd just told him had frightened the hell out of *him*.

"Of course, I'm sure about the red. Maybe it was a scarf or something, and she took it off before leaving. I don't know. But I do know I saw red. What I don't understand is why it matters so much."

He released her then, his gaze going back to the mission. "Maybe it doesn't," he muttered. "I hope like hell it doesn't."

A CHILL RIPPLED through Anna as she stared up at him. Something in his eyes, the expression on his face suddenly alarmed her. She'd said something that had made him go all moody and distant, but she had no idea what.

Help me prove Katherine Sprague was murdered.

Unbidden and unwanted, Emily Winsome's words came back to haunt Anna, and she decided it was way past time she get back to the hotel. Ben's actions were starting to make her extremely uneasy, and besides, she wanted to be alone. She needed time to think about everything that had happened today. Meeting Gwen Draven. Her dinner with Emily Winsome. And now Ben. The way he'd kissed her.... The way she'd responded....

Just thinking about it made her shiver, and she wrapped her arms around her middle. "It's getting late. I should get back, but there's no need for you to walk me the rest of the way."

"I'd prefer to," he insisted.

"But you can see the hotel lights from here," Anna protested. "If it makes you feel better, you can wait here and watch to make sure I make it back all right."

He tore his gaze from the mission to stare down at her. "Humor me. At least let me walk you to the dock."

Anna knew the dock he meant. She'd seen it from her window. A set of stone steps set into the embankment led down to it from the hotel grounds.

A few moments later, they'd reached those steps and she turned to him. "Well, here we are. I suppose I won't be seeing you again before I leave."

"No, I guess not." As if sensing the coming awkwardness, he said quickly, "I won't keep you any longer. Have a safe trip back to Houston."

"Thanks." Anna didn't linger, either, but at the top of the steps, she turned to wave a final goodbye.

But it was too late. Ben had already turned and was hurrying back along the trail toward the mission.

ANNA WAS EXHAUSTED by the time she reached her room, but she knew it was more a mental weariness than a physical one. Except for that kiss, she hadn't exactly exerted herself tonight.

But that kiss had taken a lot out of her. That kiss had scared her to death because she'd come very close to revealing everything to Ben.

And if she'd revealed her true motive for coming to San Miguel, how would he have reacted? What would he do if he found out his dead wife's heart still beat inside Anna? Would he be thankful to learn that a part of Katherine still lived on?

Or would he resent Anna for being alive? Would he begrudge her the second chance that had only been possible because of Katherine's death?

Considering the potential for an emotional and difficult confrontation, it was probably a very good thing she was returning to Houston tomorrow, Anna decided.

A knock sounded on her door just as she was slipping into her pajamas, and grabbing a robe, she hurried to the door, thinking—hoping, in spite of her misgivings—that it might be Ben.

When she opened the door, Emily Winsome gave

her an anxious smile. "I'm sorry to bother you, Anna, but I heard you come in a little while ago, and I wanted to catch you before you went to bed." Her gaze flickered over Anna's robe. "You said you'd be leaving first thing in the morning, and I was afraid I'd miss you if I waited. I have something for you." She handed Anna a book.

Anna gazed down at the cover. Ben's name was prominently displayed across the front, along with a female name in smaller letters prefaced with the caption, "In collaboration with."

The book jacket was a deep red and the title, *Deadly Seduction,* along with an embossed scorpion, were in black. A subtitle proclaimed the book "A true account of one man's obsession with a serial killer."

Anna glanced up, a sudden chill going through her.

Emily said tentatively, "You mentioned at dinner that you'd talked to someone today who'd written a book. I had a feeling you were referring to Ben Porter. I happened to own a copy of his book, and I thought you might like to have it."

"You really didn't have to do this," Anna said.

"I wanted to. Besides, I've already read it, and believe me, it's not a book I plan on reading again. It's…disturbing, to say the least. I don't recommend reading it alone after dark."

"I'll keep that in mind," Anna murmured.

"It's really too bad you're leaving so soon, or you could have him sign it for you."

Something in Emily's voice, an edge of curiosity—or was it an accusation?—made Anna wonder if the younger woman had seen her and Ben together earlier. If she might even have witnessed their kiss.

But when Anna glanced up, Emily's smile seemed guileless. "I know you're probably anxious to get to bed, but…do you think we could talk? Just for a few minutes?"

Anna hesitated. "If it concerns what we discussed at dinner, there's really nothing else to say. I can't help you, Emily. I'm sorry."

She nodded, her blue eyes round and earnest. "I understand. I do. But I don't know anyone in town I can talk to about this. Even the police aren't interested in what I have to say. If you could just…I don't know…listen to everything I've learned, let me talk it out with you, maybe it would help me put the pieces together."

Anna sighed. "I don't see how, but if you think it would help, then fine." She glanced around at the sparsely furnished space. "This room isn't exactly conducive to conversation."

"We can go outside on the balcony," Emily said eagerly. "I saw some deck chairs along the wall."

"Okay. But just for a few minutes," Anna warned. "I really do want to get an early start in the morning."

"I'll make it quick, I promise."

Once they were seated outside, however, Emily seemed reluctant to begin. She sat staring into the darkness with a brooding frown. She remained silent for so long that Anna finally turned to see what might have captured her attention. But the only movement she saw was the glitter of moonlight on the river and the sway of the Spanish moss in the breeze.

She returned her gaze to Emily. "Is something wrong? I thought you wanted to talk."

Emily didn't answer. Her stare remained fixed and unblinking as she brought her hands up to rub her arms.

Anna was puzzled by the girl's behavior. Only moments earlier, she'd been animated and eager to talk to Anna, and now it was as if she'd lapsed into an almost hypnotic trance.

An alarm bell sounded in Anna's head. Maybe letting her in hadn't been such a good idea after all. "Emily?"

She started at the sound of her name, but her gaze never left the darkness. "I'm sorry. I just...I didn't know you could see it from here."

Anna frowned. "See what?"

Emily nodded toward the river. "The old mission. I never knew you could see it from the hotel."

Anna turned and glanced toward the river where the stone ruins of the mission were hardly more than a dark silhouette against the horizon. "I spotted it today. It's beautiful, isn't it?"

"Beautiful?" At last Emily focused her gaze on Anna, her eyes gleaming eerily in the moonlight. "I don't think it's beautiful at all. I think it's a dark, evil place."

It was Anna's turn to be startled. "Why?"

"That's where it happened."

"Where what happened?"

"That's where they say Katherine committed suicide. They say she put a gun to her head and pulled the trigger, but I don't believe it. Not a word of it.''

A shudder undulated through Anna. Suddenly, she understood why Ben had been so disturbed by the sight of the mission. Why he'd been so upset when Anna had mentioned having seen someone inside earlier that day. Obviously, the ruins brought back painful memories for him.

And Emily. Her strange behavior deepened Anna's anxiety. She seemed so different tonight, so…distressed. Gone was the whimsical personality, the disarming smile, the glimmer of charm and good humor in her blue eyes. In her place was a deeply disturbed young woman who seemed obsessed with Katherine's murder.

''Who found her?'' Anna couldn't help asking.

''Her daughter, Gabriella. She was only thirteen at the time.''

''Oh, my God.''

Emily nodded. ''Yes, it was terrible. Katherine used to go to the mission when she wanted to be alone. The place held some strange fascination for her. Late that afternoon when she hadn't come home, Gabriella took a boat over to the mission to look for her. She heard the gunshot from the water, and when she rushed inside, she found Katherine covered in blood. She was still alive. Gabriella had to leave her and go back across the river for help.''

Anna closed her eyes briefly, her hand automatically going to her heart. She'd never met Katherine's daughter, knew nothing about the girl, but she ached for her just the same. Anna had also been thirteen when she'd lost her mother. Not to suicide, of course, but the tragedy had been devastating just the same. But for a child to lose her mother the way Gabriella had...to be the one to find her...

What would that do to an impressionable girl on the brink of womanhood? A difficult time under any circumstances, but to have to deal with her mother's suicide...

The death of Anna's mother had affected every aspect of her life. It had changed her in ways she was only now starting to understand. She couldn't begin to imagine how Gabriella must have been changed.

"How could she do that?" Anna murmured. "To her own child."

Emily whirled, her expression furious. "But she didn't do it! That's what I've been trying to tell you. That's what I've been trying to tell the police, but they won't listen. Katherine didn't take her own life. I know she didn't. She was too passionate about living. She wanted to experience everything. She loved trying new things, finding new thrills. She was the most *alive* person I ever knew."

And her heart still lived on inside Anna.

"There must have been an investigation into her death," Anna said.

Emily shrugged. "Oh, I'm sure they went through all the motions, but I doubt the San Miguel Police Department has much experience in investigating violent deaths, and besides, there's something about the detective who was in charge of her case that I don't trust. His name is Tony Mendoza, and he has machismo to burn. He has no regard for women, except, of course, from a purely sexual standpoint. Every time I go by the station to ask him some questions, he does nothing but stonewall. It's almost as if he's trying to cover for someone.''

''Like who?''

She didn't say anything for a moment. Then, very softly, ''When I came here looking for answers, I started with one question. Who would have the most to gain from Katherine's death?''

''That seems a logical place to start,'' Anna agreed. ''And what did you come up with?''

''The obvious.'' Emily lowered her voice. ''Katherine's husband.''

Anna's stomach knotted with dread. ''What did he have to gain from Katherine's death?''

''Everything.'' Even in the dark, Emily's gaze was very intense. ''I don't know if you're aware of this or not, but Katherine was a very wealthy woman. She inherited money when her parents were killed years ago, and then she married a rich businessman when she was only twenty-one. He died a couple of years later and left her everything.''

''Was he Gabriella's father?''

''No. Her father was a poet and songwriter, a drifter really. But he was the love of Katherine's life. When he found out she was pregnant, he stole some of her money and just took off. No one ever heard from him again.''

''How sad for Gabriella,'' Anna murmured.

''And for Katherine. She was devastated by his betrayal. I don't think there was anyone else in her life until Ben came along.'' Emily glanced away, frowning. "When she died, her estate was split between Ben and Gabriella. Ben got the house, half the money and he also oversees Gabriella's trust. In effect, he controls the whole fortune. Not bad for a former cop." Her mouth tightened, and Anna suddenly wanted to turn away from the young woman's accusing expression. She didn't want to believe Ben had anything to do with his wife's death. Not after the way he'd kissed her earlier. Not after the way she'd kissed him back...

Anna had never been one to be suckered by a handsome face, but Ben was no longer handsome. He was flawed, and somehow that made him even more attractive. And more dangerous. At least to her.

"What about Katherine's sister? How did she fare in Katherine's will?"

Emily shrugged. "Not so good. She gets to stay in the guest house for as long as she wants, and she receives a small allowance every month, but other than that, Katherine left her high and dry."

"But I was under the impression they were quite close," Anna said in surprise.

"They were at one time, but the two of them recently had a falling-out, and Katherine cut Gwen out of her will. I don't know what happened, but Katherine mentioned to me the last time we talked that she was going to have to do something about Gwen."

"What did she mean?"

Emily shrugged again. "I have no idea. All she said was that Gwen's behavior was starting to worry her, and she was going to have to do something about it."

"Do you think Gwen knew that Katherine had cut her out of her will?"

"I don't know. Why?"

"If Gwen didn't know but suspected it could happen, she might have wanted to get rid of Katherine before she had a chance to change her will."

"I never thought of that," Emily murmured.

"It's only speculation," Anna said with a shrug. "Remember, I'm going on your supposition that Katherine was murdered. I haven't seen the police reports or any of the evidence so I'm certainly not drawing that conclusion myself."

"But that's exactly why I need your help," Emily said excitedly. "You're objective. You know the right questions to ask. And you can bring a fresh eye to the investigation, not to mention a certain amount of clout. I've gotten nowhere with the police or with the D.A. But you're an attorney. Even Detective Mendoza wouldn't be able to dismiss you so easily."

Anna shook her head. "I'm sorry, but nothing you've told me tonight has made me change my mind, Emily. I'm going back to Houston first thing in the morning."

Emily studied her for a long moment. "You told me at dinner that Katherine had made a big impact on your life. So much so that you felt compelled to come here and pay your respects to her family. Don't you think you owe it to her to find out what really happened? If she was murdered, don't you think she deserves justice?"

Emily could have no idea just how effectively she was pushing Anna's buttons. Anna owed Katherine

Sprague a great deal more than anyone here could ever imagine, but she wasn't an expert in criminal law. If Katherine had been murdered, Anna wasn't the person to expose the truth.

Besides, the longer she lingered in San Miguel, the greater the risk that *she* would be exposed.

But would that be so bad?

Deep down, wasn't that what she really wanted? For Katherine's family to know that a part of her still lived on inside Anna?

Maybe that had been her original intent whether she'd admitted it to herself or not, but Anna no longer felt that way. Her whole mission had changed since she'd met Ben. She didn't want him wanting her because she had Katherine's heart. She wanted him to want her because she was Anna.

"I probably should tell you that there's someone else who had a motive," Emily said suddenly, drawing Anna out of her reverie.

Anna glanced at her, reluctant to be pulled in any further. "Who?"

"Acacia Cortina. It's pretty common knowledge around San Miguel that she has a thing for Ben and has had since he first came to town."

Anna felt a little tug at her heart, not unlike the sensation she experienced during her biopsies. Not painful, exactly, but uncomfortable nonetheless. "Does he reciprocate her feelings?"

Emily shook her head. "I have no idea. But if he and Acacia were having an affair, and Katherine found out about it—"

"Wait a minute," Anna said a bit sharply. "That's

jumping to a pretty big conclusion. You said yourself you don't know whether Ben even returned this woman's affections.''

"Okay," Emily conceded. "But even if he wasn't involved with Acacia, Ben still had a powerful motive for murder. Katherine's death made him a very rich man. In my opinion, he's still the number one suspect."

"But I understand he already had money from his book deal," Anna tried to say evenly. She didn't want Emily seeing through her, guessing that she was coming to Ben's defense so readily because she, herself, had feelings for him. "Besides, he's a former cop. He'd know how difficult it is to make murder look like suicide."

"Yes, but if anyone *could* do it and get away with it, it would be a cop," Emily returned reasonably.

"I still say you're jumping to a lot of conclusions."

Emily's enigmatic smile sent a little shiver up Anna's spine. "Read his book. Read about his obsession with a killer he called Scorpio, and then tell me if you think Ben Porter is completely sane."

ANNA ALTERNATED between tossing and turning and lying on her back, staring at the ceiling. Finally giving up any hope of sleeping, she turned on the bedside lamp and propped herself against the pillows as she reached for Ben's book.

The first line alone was enough to give her nightmares.

We were dealing with a monster. That much was evident by the way the victim had been muti-

lated. The heart had been removed from the
body. Not cleanly as a surgeon might accomplish
with a scalpel, but viciously hacked out with a
serrated knife, the kind used by butchers to cut
through bone...

Anna closed the book and set it quickly aside. She
understood now why Emily had warned her not to
read the book alone after dark. Like any good horror
tale, Ben's story had gripped Anna's spine with icy
fingers, and she knew it wouldn't let up until the very
end. And maybe not even then because unlike novels,
the events in *Deadly Seduction* were true. They'd really happened.

And if Scorpio was still alive, the ending had yet
to be written.

Chapter Eight

Anna told herself that night she wouldn't read any more of Ben's book. Not until she was back home in Houston, safe and sound in her sunny apartment with mellow music playing in the background and Laurel humming in the next room. *Deadly Seduction* was definitely not a book to be read alone in the middle of the night.

But as the minutes ticked away and she still couldn't get to sleep, she found herself reaching for the book again, and this time, she didn't put it down until just before dawn when exhaustion finally claimed her.

Surprisingly, she didn't dream about the book or have nightmares about Scorpio. If she dreamed at all, the visions were peaceful enough that they didn't wake her. When she finally opened her eyes, sunlight drifted in through the gauzy curtains at the French doors, and Anna squinted at the clock on the nightstand. It was almost nine o'clock.

She groaned and fell back against the pillows. She never slept this late, even when she'd been in her weakest condition. Her internal alarm clock always awakened her at seven o'clock sharp, still with a sense of urgency that prompted her not to linger in bed, but to get up, get showered and dressed, and get on with what had to be done.

Before she'd taken ill, Anna had prided herself on never having missed a day of work. She was always at her desk by eight, prepared for court or mediation by nine, and then after lunch would gear up for an afternoon of meetings which often ran through the dinner hour. Afterward, she would put in another few hours cleaning up paperwork so that her desk would be cleared for the start of the next day.

Often she wouldn't get home until after midnight, but she'd never complained because she knew no other way of life. She'd been driven to succeed from the time her mother died, and if Anna's heart hadn't failed her, she would have continued on in the same vein, pushing harder and harder until…

Until what? Until she'd awakened one day to find that she'd grown old all alone, that there was no one in her life who cared if she lived or died?

In a way, her heart condition had been a blessing because it made Anna realize, before it was too late, that a successful career didn't necessarily translate into a successful life. Having people that you could count on, that would always stand by you no matter what, was worth more than all the material success in the world. Laurel had taught her that.

Her life, and her outlook on life, had changed so much in the past year that Anna sometimes hardly recognized it as her own.

Rolling out of bed, she stumbled to the shower, and

thirty minutes later, dressed in jeans and a white sleeveless top, she headed downstairs to check out.

Margarete was nowhere in sight so Anna stepped up to the counter and rang the bell. After a few moments, a young woman in her late-twenties came through the arched opening behind the registration desk. She had long, dark hair, velvety brown eyes and a gorgeous body seductively displayed in white shorts and a sleeveless shirt tied underneath her full breasts.

Anna knew instantly who she was. Margarete's daughter, Acacia. The one who gave piano lessons. The one who claimed to be descended from the Mayans who'd built Chichén Itzá. The one who might or might not be having an affair with Ben.

Acacia Cortina gave Anna a quick once-over, then obviously concluding she constituted little or no threat, smiled warmly. "May I help you?"

Anna set her bag on the floor. "I'm checking out of Room 209."

"I hope you've enjoyed your stay," the woman said as she rifled through a file box underneath the counter. "You said 209, right? I can't seem to find…oh, here it is." She withdrew a registration slip and glanced up with a slight frown. "Anna Sebastian?"

"Yes, that's right."

Acacia slid the credit card slip across the desk. "If you'll just sign the receipt, you'll be all set to go."

"Thanks." Anna scribbled her name on the form, aware all the while that Acacia Cortina's gaze was still on her. Anna knew why she was curious about

Acacia, but she had no idea why the other woman suddenly found her so interesting.

"If you'll wait here, I'll have Amador bring your car around to the front."

"No, don't bother. I'll find it."

"In that case, have a safe trip back to Houston."

Anna was halfway out the door before she stopped and glanced around, wondering how Acacia knew her destination was Houston. From her address in the registration book? Or had Ben said something to her?

It gave Anna a funny feeling to think that she might be the topic of one of his conversations. Had he even thought about her since last night? Had he thought about their kiss?

That kiss.

Just the thought of his lips on hers, his hands moving over her body, made Anna tingle all over. She'd never responded that way to a kiss. With total abandon. With wanton disregard for the consequences. She'd wanted him, so much so at that moment she'd been willing to forget who he was and why she'd come to San Miguel. She'd been willing to ignore the fact that his wife's heart beat inside her chest and if he knew...

If he knew...

She drew a breath as she walked out into the hot, brilliant day. He wasn't going to know. Not unless he chose to. If he responded to the letter the hospital had sent anonymously on her behalf, if he made the request to meet her, then and only then would Anna tell him the truth. Until that time, she'd go back to Houston and get on with her life, and she'd let Ben do the same. She'd come here for her own peace of mind, but it wouldn't be fair to destroy his in the process.

After stowing her bag in the trunk, Anna opened the car door and climbed in. The interior was like a furnace. She left the door open to release the stale, hot air while she inserted her key into the ignition and turned it.

Nothing happened.

She turned the key again and pumped the gas a little. Still nothing. Not so much as a click.

Popping the hood, she got out of the car to have a look even though she hadn't the foggiest idea what she was looking for. She remembered once when her dad's car had had a similar problem, he'd gotten the engine to turn over by cleaning the corrosion off the battery posts. But as Anna peered under the hood, she realized she had no idea where her battery was even located. It wasn't in a prominent position the way the battery had been in her dad's car.

As she gazed helplessly at the mass of wires and hoses, a shadow fell across the car and she turned to find Amador standing just behind her. He nodded, and the silver cross in his ear flashed brilliantly in the sunlight as he stepped up to the car.

"No start?"

Anna shook her head. "I think I may have a dead battery. Is there a garage nearby where I could get someone to give me a jump?"

"Un segundo por favor." He strode toward an old battered pickup truck that had been parked in the shade of an elm tree. Cranking the ancient engine, he maneuvered the truck around to the front of Anna's

car and then set to work with jumper cables he'd pulled from underneath the truck seat.

But after ten minutes and still no luck, he stood back, scratching his head in defeat. "My cousin owns a *garaje* in town. We call him."

Anna had no choice but to agree. She waited on the front steps of the hotel for Amador's cousin, Luis, and then a few minutes later, watched with trepidation as he towed her car away with a wrecker that looked as if it might not make it to the end of the drive. But Luis seemed to have a good deal more faith than Anna. He gave her a saucy salute as he chugged down the drive toward the street.

"Anna?"

She turned as Emily, dressed in white Capri pants and sneakers, came out of the hotel and ran lightly down the steps. "I thought you'd be almost home by now." She slipped on her sunglasses. "What happened?"

Anna pointed toward the wrecker that was just disappearing down the street. "My car wouldn't start. I had to have it towed to a garage."

"You're kidding!" Emily plopped down on the steps beside her. "If that isn't serendipity, I don't know what is. There I was trying my hardest last night to convince you to stay and help me with my investigation, and now it seems you have no choice."

Something in her tone touched a nerve. Anna glanced at her sharply, a suspicion bubbling to the surface. Was it possible her car trouble was something slightly more diabolical than mere bad luck?

It was probably her imagination, Anna told herself, but Emily's smile looked a tad smug this morning.

"If it's nothing too serious, I can still leave today," Anna said testily. "I haven't changed my mind since last night."

Emily seemed to sense it was time to back off. "Okay. I understand."

"But I have been thinking about everything you told me." Anna watched the street for a moment, then turned to Emily. "If Katherine Sprague really was murdered as you seem so convinced she was, then this investigation of yours could be dangerous. You do realize that, don't you?"

Emily's blue eyes flickered. "You mean because her killer might come after me? I've thought about that. But I don't think he'd dare. If anything happened to me, it would prove Katherine was murdered, wouldn't it?"

"Unless it was made to look like an accident."

Emily shook her head. "I still say he wouldn't risk it. Not after all this time. He must think he's gotten away with it."

The way she kept using the male pronoun for the killer unnerved Anna. It was obvious Ben was still her number one suspect, and Anna was almost tempted to help with the misguided investigation just to prove her wrong.

But was it Emily she wanted to convince of Ben's innocence…or herself?

EMILY GAVE ANNA a ride to the garage later that morning on her way out of town. She was meeting some friends for lunch in San Antonio, and then afterward, she wanted to do some research at the University of St. Agnes library. She assured Anna she'd be back by dinner and tried to get her to ride along, but Anna declined, not overly anxious to continue their previous conversation.

She preferred instead to concentrate on Luis's preliminary diagnosis of her car. After his complicated and rather lengthy explanation in both English and Spanish, she still had only a vague notion that the problem had something to do with the alternator and could be fixed in a matter of hours if Luis could find the right part. But finding the right part was no simple matter. Not in San Miguel. Luis had made phone calls. Lots of phone calls. *Nada.* No luck. If the part had to be ordered from Germany, it would take weeks to arrive.

"From Germany!" Anna said in astonishment. "That car is only three years old. Surely someone somewhere in Texas stocks parts for it."

No worries, Luis assured her. He had a cousin in the valley who owned a salvage yard. He might be able to get the part from him.

Anna sighed in frustration. "Is there someplace in town where I can rent a vehicle?" If she was going to be stuck in San Miguel for the next couple of days, she didn't want to be without transportation.

Luis beamed and led her over to a bay in the garage where he proudly unveiled a candy-apple-red Mustang convertible. The car was at least thirty years old and looked every minute of it, but the battered muscle car was obviously his pride and joy.

"Twenty-five dollars a day. You buy the gas. That's a good deal, no?"

Anna nodded and took out her wallet. "You take VISA?"

"VISA, MasterCard, American Express. Just like in the big city." He grinned and plucked her platinum card from her fingers without the slightest hesitation.

Anna couldn't help but return his smile. Unlike the dour Amador, Cousin Luis was a real charmer.

He opened the door for her, and when Anna climbed inside, he bent to peer down at her. "You drive a stick, no?"

Anna glanced doubtfully at the stick shift. It had been years since she'd driven a car with a standard transmission, but she hoped it was like riding a bike. It would all come back to her once she started the engine.

But it proved a little more difficult than riding a bike. After a couple of false starts and some grinding of gears, Anna finally managed to ease the car from its slot in the garage. As she pulled onto the street, she glanced in the rearview mirror. Luis stood on the sidewalk anxiously watching her, and as she narrowly missed sideswiping a minivan, she saw him lift a hand to quickly cross himself.

WHAT POSSESSED HER to drive across the river and locate the old mission, Anna couldn't honestly say. She'd only meant to cruise around town for a few minutes to get her bearings before heading back to the hotel to check in again.

But then, all of a sudden, the old metal bridge

which spanned the river rose in front of her, and before Anna realized what she was doing, she'd driven across and headed north on a narrow, paved lane heavily overhung with the drooping branches of live oaks.

The mission was less than a half mile from the bridge, and as Ben had said the evening before, the road led right to it.

Anna was surprised that no other cars were about as she pulled to the side of the road. She wasn't certain what she'd been expecting. Tourists milling about grounds as lush and manicured as those surrounding the Alamo maybe. But instead, the place was deserted, the atmosphere slightly oppressive beneath a heavy canopy of leaves that blocked the sunlight.

Part of the stone wall that had once protected the mission from incursions by the French and by marauding Apache and Comanche war parties had long since crumbled away, and the rest was covered with a thick blanket of lichen.

A squirrel rummaged in the underbrush, and Anna paused, watching the swish of his tail, the avid dart of his beady little eyes as he scrambled through the dead leaves. Then he was gone, lost from her sight as he scurried up a tree.

As Anna turned back to the mission, she saw a movement out of the corner of her eye. Another squirrel, she told herself, but the motion had come from inside the mission. She glanced up at the high stone facade, shivering, even though the day was hot and humid.

It was strange, but she wasn't frightened. Not really. What she felt instead of fear was a nagging uneasiness that perhaps she shouldn't be there and a vague sense of déjà vu that made her wonder if she'd already *been* there. But she knew she hadn't. She'd never set foot in San Miguel before yesterday.

There was a perfectly logical explanation for the déjà vu, she told herself. The familiarity of the place probably stemmed from her visits to the other missions along the San Antonio River.

When her mother had been alive, they'd often gone to San Antonio to spend weekends. They'd dine on the River Walk, shop at the exotic El Mercado and toured the missions, always a highlight for Anna's mother.

Now, as Anna stood gazing at the Mission San Miguel, those memories came flooding back. For the first time in years, she let herself remember her mother, really remember her, and an aching loneliness swept over her. She could almost hear her mother's soft laughter, her lilting voice as she recounted the missions' rich history.

Making her way inside the walls, Anna opened the heavy wooden door and stepped inside. She'd expected the interior to be dark and dank, but sunlight streamed in from openings placed high on the stone wall near the roofline.

The muscles in her chest tightened painfully as she looked around. This was where it had happened. This was where Katherine Sprague's life had ended, and Anna's second chance had begun.

Technically, of course, Katherine's life had ended in the hospital, when life support had been terminated.

But inside the mission, perhaps in this very room, was where she'd made the decision not to go on.

Or where someone else had made that decision for her.

The dirt floor was so uneven in places that Anna stumbled once or twice as she wandered around. And suddenly, as she lingered inside, she began to get a very bad feeling about the mission. What was it Emily had said last night? *I don't think it's beautiful at all. I think it's a dark, evil place.*

Yes, Anna thought, with a cold, spine-tingling shiver. Evil had been there. She could feel it. She'd experienced a similar uncanny chill the first time she'd entered the Alamo, but there was a subtle difference here. She couldn't explain it, but she was suddenly very afraid.

She whirled to leave, but someone blocked her way. Someone who had come in so silently, Anna hadn't heard his approach. Someone who might still have murder in his heart...

SHE JUMPED BACK and stumbled on the uneven floor. Ben reached out to steady her, but the moment he touched her, she started so violently, he let his hands drop from her arms immediately. He stared down at her with a frown. "What are you doing here?"

Her hand crept to her throat. Ben thought he could see it tremble. "I could ask you the same thing."

"I came to see if I could figure out who was over here yesterday. You said you saw someone, remember?"

She nodded. "I did see someone. But I still don't understand why it matters."

Ben shrugged. "Maybe it doesn't. But I thought I'd have a look around anyway. It'd be a shame if vandals destroyed this place."

Anna lowered her voice, her gaze moving to the stone steps that led to the bell tower. "I saw something earlier when I first got here. I wondered if someone was up there."

Ben lifted a brow, but didn't say anything. Instead he glanced quickly around, then leaned forward and said very softly against Anna's ear, "Wait here. I'll have a look around."

She nodded, but she looked as if she might bolt at any moment. Ben wondered what had shaken her up so badly. And why the hell she'd come here in the first place.

He searched through all the rooms and then climbed the steps to the bell tower. If anyone had recently been in the mission, they were long gone now.

He came back down the steps to join Anna. "No one's here. Are you sure you didn't see a squirrel?"

She frowned. "It…might have been."

"Sometimes a place like this can play tricks on the imagination."

She nodded vaguely, but didn't agree or dispute him. Instead she glanced around, lifting her hands to rub her arms as if suddenly chilled.

He felt the same way. "Let's get out of here," he muttered.

He led them outside to a low stone wall that overlooked the river. They both sat down, and after a moment, when the eeriness of the mission began to fade, he said, "What are you still doing in San Miguel? Last night you said you were leaving first thing this morning for Houston."

"I had car trouble." She turned her dark gaze to his, and something stirred to life inside Ben. Passion, yes, the kind they'd experienced last night across the river. But something else, too. Something he didn't want to put a name to.

A mild breeze drifted up from the water, lifting a strand of her blond hair, then settling it artfully back into place. She'd pulled her hair back today in the way she'd worn it the first time he saw her. The style that made her look elegant and sophisticated. Cool and unapproachable. Untouchable.

Last night she'd worn it down, and it was as if freeing her hair had unleashed something wild inside her. Something needy and desperate. Something that made Ben go hot at the thought of being in bed with her.

He wished liked hell he knew what she was thinking. She had a great poker face, one that had probably served her very well in the courtroom.

"Is something wrong?" she asked softly.

Her voice did all kinds of bad things to his insides. To his mind. To his resolve. "No," he lied. "Why?"

"You seem so...preoccupied." She glanced toward the mission. "This place must hold a lot of bad memories for you."

"Then you know what happened here," he said grimly.

She nodded. "I can't imagine what it must be like for you, coming back here to the place where it happened. How can you stand to be here?" Her gaze took on a glint that Ben thought was slightly accusing.

He frowned. "It's just a place."

"I know, but still..." She shuddered. "You lost someone here that you loved."

He glanced away from her piercing eyes to stare at the river. "Maybe I should explain something about Katherine and me...about our relationship." He turned back to Anna. "I didn't love her. I never loved her. Toward the end, I came to despise her."

Chapter Nine

Those words, spoken in such a calm voice, chilled Anna to the bone.

Despised her?

He'd despised Katherine? Anna closed her eyes briefly, trying to let his words sink in.

"But you must have loved her when you married her," she finally said. "Gwen called it love at first sight. She said the two of you couldn't keep your hands off each other."

He grimaced as his gaze went back to the river. "The thought of touching her, of ever having touched her, makes my skin crawl."

Somehow his pronouncement was like a dagger through Anna's heart. He wasn't talking about her, and yet she felt as if he was. He hadn't betrayed her, and yet it seemed as if he had. An unreasonable anger welled inside her, and she had to struggle very hard to keep it subdued. "Then why did you marry her?"

He paused. "It's hard to explain."

"Was it her money?" The bitterness in her voice shocked Anna. She had no right to feel this way. No *reason* to feel this way, but she couldn't seem to help herself. Why had he married Katherine if he hadn't loved her? Why had he kissed Anna if...

The two events were not the same. She was *not* Katherine.

But she had Katherine's heart. It was beating inside her chest at that very moment.

The thought of touching her, of ever having touched her, makes my skin crawl.

Would he feel the same about Anna if he knew? Would he despise her, too? Would he be unable and unwilling to ever touch her again?

"It wasn't the money," Ben said.

"Then what was it?"

"Lust, I guess." He ran a hand through his hair. "But it was more complicated than that. Katherine was a difficult woman to know. People either adored her or hated her. There was no middle ground with her. And the people who loved her the most, often ended up despising her. She had a way of using up the best in people and then discarding them like yesterday's trash."

"If you felt that way about her, why didn't you leave her?" Anna asked.

He stared at the river with a brooding frown. "I wanted to, but there was Gabby to consider. She'd formed an attachment to me by then, and the poor kid had a hard enough time with a mother like Katherine. I couldn't just walk away."

"But some people might say she wasn't your responsibility," Anna said carefully.

Ben's jaw tightened. "Gabby became my respon-

sibility the day I married her mother. If I learned anything as a cop it's that you don't walk out on a kid.''

Anna thought of all the custody cases she'd argued
in which the children had been nothing more than
pawns in the divorcing couple's ongoing battle. She
was suddenly, deeply ashamed that she'd played any
part in tearing a child's life apart.

''Hey, are you okay?'' Ben put a hand on her arm,
and Anna jumped. She couldn't help it. Even so slight
a touch from him had a powerful effect on her.

His features tightened at her reaction. ''Sorry.''

''No, it's okay. I'm just…a bit jumpy.'' She
shrugged. ''It's this place…what you just told me…''

''I never should have said anything. I keep forgetting you're a stranger.''

His gaze deepened, and Anna's stomach fluttered
in awareness. ''I know,'' she said softly. ''I feel the
same way. But I don't understand why.''

He didn't respond but his gaze was all over her.
Anna could tell that he wanted her as much as she
wanted him, and that was the strangest part of this
whole strange situation. She knew she was still an
attractive woman in spite of everything she'd been
through, but she'd never possessed that intangible
quality that brought out the pure animal lust in men.

Judging by her photographs, Katherine had had that
quality in abundance. Acacia Cortina had it, too. But
Anna didn't. She'd never been the type of woman
who was driven by her sexual urges, and men picked
up on that. Men were put off by that. She enjoyed
sex, she supposed, but she never particularly craved
it. Had never been the one to initiate lovemaking even

during her short marriage. Her lack of ardor had been
a frequent complaint of Hays's.

But with Ben…

Anna could feel something building inside her just
looking at him. With Ben, she was ready to throw
caution to the wind for the first time in her life. She
was almost—but not quite—ready to initiate sex with
a man who was a virtual stranger.

"What are you thinking?" His gaze was deep and
knowing.

Anna had to glance away so he couldn't see the
truth. "I was thinking about what you just said. People either loved or hated Katherine. If she aroused
such strong emotions in the people around her, do you
think it's possible…" She trailed away.

"What? Go ahead and say it."

"Do you think it's possible that someone was here
with her that day? Maybe she didn't take her own
life."

Anna thought that he would be shocked by her suggestion, but instead he merely glanced at her.
"You've been talking to Emily Winsome, I see."

Anna was the one who was surprised. "You know
her?"

"I've met her a few times. She was one of Katherine's groupies."

"Groupies?"

"For lack of a better word. Every year Katherine
picked one or two of her students to mentor. But she
was more than just an adviser to them. She became
their guru. They came to her with all their problems.
Hung on her every word. They worshipped the

ground she walked on. And she would invite them here to spend summers with her. Her retreat, she called it, although I never was too clear on what they studied.''

"And Emily was one of Katherine's...protégées?''

He nodded. "The students would stay in one of the guest cottages out back, but they pretty much had the run of the place.''

"How did Gwen feel about these retreats? You told me yesterday that she resented your marriage to Katherine because it took her sister's time and attention away from her. What about Katherine's students? Didn't Gwen mind the time and attention Katherine gave to them?''

"Not at first. She used to be a part of Katherine's inner circle, but then later, when she and Katherine started having problems, she became little more than a glorified secretary.''

"How did she feel about that?''

"Knowing Gwen, she resented the hell out of it, but Katherine controlled the purse strings. She didn't have a choice but to do as Katherine said.''

"Couldn't she have gotten a job?'' Anna asked. "Moved out on her own?''

Ben gave a sharp laugh. "Gwen has never worked a day in her life. She has no idea how to function in the real world. Katherine saw to that.''

What a strange family, Anna thought. "Emily told me that Gwen and Katherine had a falling-out before she died. She said Katherine cut Gwen out of her will. Is that true?''

He nodded. "Pretty much. She gets an allowance, enough to get by on, but that's about it."

"Do you think Gwen knew that Katherine had changed her will before she died?"

His gaze met hers. "You're pretty quick, aren't you?"

Anna shrugged. "Money has always been a powerful motivation for murder."

"Then you must also know that when Katherine cut Gwen out, she divided her estate between Gabby and me."

"Yes, I do know that," Anna said. "But you didn't kill her."

He turned at that. "What makes you so certain? You hardly know me."

She shrugged again. "I don't know how I know it, but I do. If I thought there was the slightest chance you'd murdered your wife, do you think I'd be here with you now?" She waved a hand toward the mission. "Here, of all places."

"Why *are* you here, Anna?" His gaze was so deeply compelling, she couldn't look away. She could lose herself in those eyes, she thought, and become…whatever he wanted her to be.

"I was drawn here," she said helplessly. "I had to come."

"Because you think Katherine was murdered?"

"I don't know. Emily seems convinced of it. She said that Katherine wasn't the type to commit suicide."

He fell silent for a moment. "Did Emily also tell you that she was in love with Katherine?"

Anna stared at him in shock. "In love with her?"

"She became obsessed with her after the summer she stayed with her. That was before I came here, but even after Katherine and I married, Emily would still call at all hours. Drop by without notice. Katherine thought her devotion was amusing for a while, but then she got bored with her. She even took out a restraining order against Emily."

"Oh, my God. How did Emily react to that?"

"Not well," Ben said with a grimace. "She was just a kid infatuated with an older teacher. When she told Katherine how she felt, Katherine laughed in her face. Emily was devastated. She threatened to kill Katherine and then take her own life." His gaze met Anna's in the mottled sunlight. "But I bet she didn't bother telling you that, either, did she?"

ANNA WAS RELIEVED when Emily didn't show up for dinner in the dining room that night. She still wasn't certain how she wanted to handle the information Ben had given her earlier. Her first instinct was to ignore it and not get any more caught up in Emily's claim that Katherine had been murdered than she already was.

But it bothered her that Emily had come to her for help without being honest about her own involvement with Katherine. She should have told Anna about the threats and the restraining order because withholding the information now made her look as if she had something to hide.

Still, Anna had a hard time imagining Emily as a killer. And if she had murdered Katherine, why would

she be here now, in San Miguel, stirring up the proverbial hornet's nest? To throw off suspicion? Why
would she need to? Katherine's death had been ruled
a suicide. Legally speaking, the case was closed.

No, Anna just couldn't see Emily as the killer—if
there had indeed *been* a killer. But it was ironic, she
supposed, that Emily and Ben had pointed the finger
at each other.

Why Anna had decided to accept Ben's word about
Emily's infatuation with Katherine without corrobo-
ration, she wasn't quite sure. But where her feelings
for Ben were concerned, she wasn't certain of anything. Her intense attraction to him made no sense,
but it was there all the same, real and so powerful it
took her breath away just to look at him.

With no plans for the evening, Anna went straight
up to her room after dinner. It was too early to sleep,
but she got ready for bed anyway. Slipping between
the covers, she propped herself against the pillows
and reached for Ben's book.

She'd gotten well past the halfway mark the night
before, and the disturbing images of the murders he'd
painted so graphically had been floating around in the
back of her mind all day. The victims—all women—
were killed with a bullet wound to the head, but before their executions, they'd been tortured. The hearts
had been removed postmortem, but for what purpose,
no one knew. None of the organs had ever been
found, but that sort of mutilation was usually indic-
ative of a ritual-style killing.

Anna's stomach churned as she continued to read.

She learned things she didn't want to know but would never forget.

Yet as unsettling as the book was, she couldn't put it down because it also gave her an amazing insight into Ben's psyche—not so much for what he said about himself, but for what he didn't say.

He didn't dwell on his own personal ordeal with Scorpio, but Anna could read between the lines. And she remembered what Gwen had told her that first day in San Miguel. *The scars on his hand and face... Scorpio did that to him. And the scars on the inside are even worse. I don't think Ben ever recovered from that summer.*

Long after Anna had finished the book and set it aside, she lay in the darkness of her room, staring at the ceiling and trying to imagine what that summer must have done to Ben. What it had cost him.

For that whole summer—and ever since, Anna suspected—the case had been his whole life. He'd lived, breathed, dreamed of bringing a brutal serial killer to justice. And when he awakened one night to find Scorpio in his apartment, his determination and dedication had become an obsession.

Before Scorpio, Ben had been a high-profile cop, the one reporters went to for interviews and expert analysis of crime scenes because he was not only knowledgeable, but highly personable and photogenic. The cameras loved him. He was destined to go all the way to the top in the Houston Police Department.

But Scorpio ended all that. Scorpio took everything from him—his looks, his career, very nearly his life.

And what the killer left behind was a haunted man. A man who couldn't put the past behind him because it was there, in front of him, each and every time he looked in the mirror.

ANNA DIDN'T THINK she'd be able to sleep at all that night, but sometime after midnight, she finally drifted off, only to come awake suddenly at a noise somewhere nearby.

She lay very still, listening to the night, telling herself the sound had been a dream. But as she huddled underneath the covers, the noise came again. Floorboards creaked in the hallway outside her room. The hotel was either settling or someone was walking past her door.

Anna's first thought was that perhaps Emily had returned from San Antonio much later than she'd planned. Or maybe the other guest—Dwight Gump— had come in from the field, although Emily had said his room was in the other wing. Maybe he was disoriented, drunk...

Maybe it was Acacia. Or Margarete.

Or Scorpio...

Anna pulled the covers up to her chin, all the while telling herself she was letting her imagination get the better of her. But she couldn't stop trembling. And she couldn't stop the images of Scorpio's victims flashing strobelike through her head.

Finally, unable to stand the suspense any longer, she got up quietly and started across the room. When the boards screeched beneath her feet, she stopped. Outside, the creaking ceased.

If someone was out there, they'd undoubtedly heard the noise from inside her room and knew that she was up and about. And now they were out there, listening to the quiet, just as she was doing in her room. It was almost as if the two of them were holding a collective breath.

Then, in one swift movement, Anna crossed the floor and pressed her ear to the door. Nothing moved. Nothing creaked. If someone had been out there, they were probably long gone by now.

Or still out there, waiting, daring her to make the next move.

Anna wasn't about to open the door and find out.

Turning back to the bed, she caught a movement out of the corner of her eye. A shadow crept along the balcony and then was gone.

A surge of adrenaline caused her heart to knock painfully against her chest. She didn't know what to do. She was trapped between the creaking floorboards in the hallway and the shadow on the balcony. She couldn't open either door to escape.

The notion flitted through her head that she should call down to the desk for help. But...did the Casa del Gatos even have a night clerk? Anna had no idea if anyone would even be about at this hour to take her call.

The police then? Or Ben?

And tell them what? That she was hearing and seeing things after reading a book about a serial killer? Floorboards in a one-hundred-year-old hotel were suddenly creaking. A shadow had moved on her balcony.

Anna laughed nervously, the sound startling in the silence. Okay, so her imagination was running away with her.

Check the locks on both doors, she told herself, and go back to bed. There was nothing to worry about. Nothing to be afraid of.

But once she was settled in bed again, she didn't dare close her eyes until the gray light of dawn filtered in through the windows.

THE NEXT MORNING, it seemed obvious that the culprit had indeed been an overwrought imagination. Anna showered quickly and dressed, and decided her first order of business would be to check in with Luis about her car.

Depending on what he told her, she might have to do some shopping or find a laundry. She'd already gone through all the clothes she'd brought for an overnight stay, and in this heat, plenty of fresh clothing was a necessity.

As she left her room, Anna's gaze went to the door across the hall. She started to go over and knock, but then decided that if it had been Emily getting in late the night before, it wouldn't be polite to disturb her so early.

Besides, with the sun already shining relentlessly overhead, the shadows and nightmares fled.

Anna drove with the top down in spite of the heat, and when she arrived at the garage, Luis met her with good and bad news. He'd located a part. It was being expressed from Dallas, but since the following day was Sunday, the part wouldn't arrive until Monday.

It could be as late as Tuesday before he had her car running, which meant that Anna could be stranded in San Miguel for another four days unless she wanted to return to Houston without her car.

But since she didn't have any commitments in the city until a scheduled biopsy at the end of the following week, she didn't think it would make sense to drive all that way only to have to turn around and come back once her car was repaired.

At least that was what she told herself.

Ben, of course, had nothing to do with her decision to stay.

Two hours later, arms loaded with shopping bags, Anna returned to the hotel. As she inserted her key into the lock, she glanced across the hall. Emily's door was still closed, but Anna knew the younger woman was probably up and about by now.

Dropping her packages inside her own room, Anna stepped across the hall and knocked. To her surprise, the door creaked open, and she cautiously peered inside.

The place was a mess. Contents of drawers had been dumped on the floor, the pillows and mattress were slashed to ribbons, and the lining of Emily's suitcase had been ripped out and shredded.

Someone had gone after the room with a vengeance. And suddenly Anna experienced the same sensation she'd had in the mission—that dark, creeping certainty that she was in the presence of evil.

Backing out of the room, she turned and fled through the hallway and down the stairs.

Chapter Ten

Anna was waiting for Ben in the lobby when he arrived.

She rose from a carved bench and hurried toward him. "Thanks for coming."

"No problem. You sounded pretty upset on the phone." Although she seemed much calmer and in control now, Ben noticed.

"It was a shock to see Emily's room like that. Come on. I'll show you."

They started toward the stairs.

"Has anyone gone up there since you called me?" Ben asked.

She paused. "I did, but I didn't touch anything."

He scowled down at her. "I asked you to wait down here for me."

"I know, but I was afraid Emily might be up there, hurt or…worse, and needed medical attention."

"And?"

Anna shook her head. "I didn't see any sign of her, but, Ben, I'm still really worried about her. She said she'd be back by dinnertime last night, and she never arrived. And now this…"

"Did you call the police?"

"Margarete did. They should be here soon."

Ben took Anna's elbow as they climbed the stairs, all the while telling himself he was a fool for touching her. Probably a fool for rushing over here the way he had, but once he'd heard the fear in her tone, nothing could have kept him away. And that worried him, too.

She led him to the end of the hallway and pointed to the door on the right. "This is her room."

The door was still ajar, and with his foot, Ben edged it open a little farther. Even from the doorway, he could tell Anna's concern was justified. Someone had really done a number on Emily Winsome's room.

He glanced over his shoulder. "Wait out here."

Slowly, he entered the room, taking care where he stepped and making sure he didn't touch anything, either. He checked under the bed, in the closet, and then in the bathroom. No body, no blood, no sign of a struggle that Ben could discern. That was good news, at least.

He took another moment to glance around, then walked back out to the hallway.

Anna said anxiously, "What do you think?"

He shrugged. "Hard to say. It's possible the police can get some prints, but I'm not holding my breath."

Anna ran her hands up and down her arms, as if suddenly chilled. "When I first saw the way her room had been trashed, I thought someone must have been looking for something. Money or jewelry. But that's not it, is it? Whoever did this was in a rage. Or else they wanted to scare her."

Or they were acting out, Ben thought grimly. The

destruction to Emily Winsome's room was overkill. An intruder looking for valuables wouldn't have taken the time to tear apart pillows or shred every article of clothing that had been hanging in the closet.

Even her underwear had been slashed to ribbons.

Anna was right. The destruction here was personal, and Ben's gut instinct told him that she was right about something else, too. Emily Winsome could be in big trouble.

But he kept his fears to himself. He didn't want to worry Anna any more than she obviously already was. He tried to push away the protective instincts that were struggling to the surface. Tried to tell himself that Anna Sebastian wasn't his problem.

But when he turned and gazed down into her upturned face, he suddenly wanted nothing more than to take her in his arms and hold on to her until he could be sure she was safe.

The time for that, however, would have to be later. They both turned as footsteps sounded down the hallway. Tony Mendoza, flanked on either side by Margarete and Acacia Cortina, strode toward them.

Mendoza wasn't a tall man, but what he lacked in stature, he made up for in bravado. Dressed in jeans, boots and a black T-shirt, his long, black hair greased back and fastened in a ponytail, he looked more like a street thug than a cop.

As he neared the room, his gaze zeroed in on Anna and lingered. Lingered for so long, in fact, that Ben moved to her side. The possessive gesture was not lost on Mendoza, who smirked, nor on Acacia. Her dark eyes narrowed as she glanced from Ben to Anna, then back to Ben.

Ben had a sinking feeling that trouble was brewing inside her mercenary little heart.

Mendoza strode to Emily's room and glanced inside. "Has anyone been in here since I was called?" he demanded.

"Both Anna and I had a quick look around to make sure no one had been hurt, but nothing has been disturbed."

Mendoza turned with a scowl. "What are you even doing here, Porter?"

Before Ben could answer, Anna said, "I called and asked him to come."

Mendoza gave Anna another once-over, this one not quite as friendly as the first. "And you are?"

"Anna Sebastian. I'm the one who discovered the room."

"And so you just strolled right on in, huh? It never even occurred to you that the intruder might still be in there?"

"It did," Anna admitted. "But I was worried about Emily. I thought she might be hurt."

Mendoza turned to Ben. "And your excuse?"

Ben shrugged. "The same."

"So it took the two of you to figure out that Emily Winsome wasn't in there. Interesting." His gaze was still on Ben. "You seem to have a bad habit of turning up at crime scenes, Porter. I'm starting to get a little curious about that."

"You know what they say about curiosity," Ben said.

Mendoza didn't seem to appreciate Ben's irony. "By all rights, I could haul you in for tampering with evidence."

Ben was used to Mendoza's threats, but he could tell Anna was taken aback by the man's posturing.

"Now wait just a minute," she said.

And she was clearly not going to let him get away with it.

Ben watched with amusement as her cheeks flushed with color and her eyes snapped with anger. He had a feeling he was glimpsing a bit of the woman Anna had been before her illness. "Ben's here because I asked him to come. I had no idea when you would get here, Detective, and I was very worried that something had happened to Emily Winsome. For all we knew, she could have been lying in that room, hurt or even dead. We had to check it out. So your attitude, as far as I can tell, is completely unwarranted."

Mendoza lifted a brow. "You're very quick to rush to Porter's defense, Ms. Sebastian. Maybe you didn't have to call him over here at all."

Anna frowned. "What do you mean?"

"Maybe," Mendoza said softy, "He was already here."

A subtle change came over Anna. She suddenly looked pretty damn intimidating in her own right. "I really don't see how that's any of your business."

"It's my business if Porter was here at the time of the break-in." He returned Anna's frosty stare. "Are you aware that Emily Winsome believed Porter's wife was murdered?"

"Yes. But—"

Ben saw the exact moment when Mendoza's subtle inference hit her. She hid her shock well, though, behind her icy facade. "Are you suggesting the break-in has something to do with Katherine's murder?"

Mendoza glanced at Ben. "Why don't we ask Porter what he thinks?"

Ben shrugged. "You're the one who determined Katherine's death was a suicide."

"Yes," Mendoza agreed. "But that's one case I've never quite been able to close the book on."

"If you think there was some justification to Emily's claim, why didn't you cooperate with her?" Anna demanded. "She said you blew her off every time she tried to talk to you."

"Maybe I didn't want her stumbling into something she couldn't handle." Mendoza glanced back at Emily's room. "But it appears she managed to get herself into trouble anyway."

Anna's gaze met Ben's, and he wondered if that was doubt he saw flickering in her eyes. Doubt and suspicion. Two emotions Ben knew only too well.

Mendoza turned to Margarete and Acacia, who'd been hovering on the fringes of the conversation, silent but certainly not disinterested. "Are there any other guests registered in the hotel besides Ms. Sebastian and Ms. Winsome?"

"Mr. Gump is in the other wing." Margarete's disapproving gaze flashed briefly to Anna, as if to let her know she didn't appreciate having this trouble brought down on her. "But he wasn't in last night. He's been out of town for over a week. We had another gentlemen check in late last night. A Mr. Carter. He's also in the other wing.''

"Which room?''

"I put him in 203, but he's not in. He left early this morning, and I don't know when he'll be back.''

Mendoza turned to Anna. "Where's your room?''

Anna pointed across the hall. "I'm in 209.''

"Directly across from Ms. Winsome's room.'' Mendoza rubbed his chin. "And you didn't hear anything last night? No unusual noises? Nothing?''

"I thought I heard someone walking around out in the hallway at one point.''

"What time was that?''

"Just after three. I woke up and heard the floorboards creaking outside my room. I thought maybe Emily was just getting in.''

Ben stared at her in surprise. Why hadn't she told him about this earlier?

"You didn't look out to see if it was her?'' Mendoza queried.

Anna hesitated. Her gaze flashed to Ben's. "I decided it was just the hotel settling.''

"Is there any possibility that the intruder may have been looking for your room?'' Mendoza asked suddenly.

Anna stared at him in shock, as if the idea had never occurred to her.

It hadn't occurred to Ben, either, until that moment.

AFTER MENDOZA LEFT, Ben and Anna walked outside and found a shady bench that overlooked the river and sat down. Anna stared at the water for a moment, then sensing Ben's gaze on her, she turned. He reached over and tucked a strand of hair behind her ear, and the tenderness of the gesture made Anna long for something she'd never had and wasn't even sure existed.

"You look tired this morning," he murmured.

She couldn't remember the last time someone other than Laurel had sounded so concerned about her. "I didn't get much sleep last night."

"Creaking floorboards kept you awake?"

Anna glanced away. "Something like that."

"Why didn't you tell me you thought you heard someone outside your room last night?"

"Because I didn't think it was important. I thought it was just my imagination."

"You don't seem the type to let your imagination run away with you," Ben said.

Anna shrugged. "When you're in a strange town, a strange room..." *And you've just read a book about a serial killer...* "You hear things, see things."

"*See* things? Like what?"

Anna hesitated. "I thought I saw a shadow out on the balcony last night."

"Why didn't you call me?" he demanded.

"Because I didn't think it was anything," she insisted. "Look, I really think the person we need to be worried about right now is Emily. What if Mendoza is right, Ben? What if her disappearance has something to do with Katherine's murder?"

He frowned and abruptly turned to scowl at the river.

"I don't think you had anything to do with it,"

Anna said softly. "I know that was Mendoza's insinuation, but I don't believe it."

He turned and gave her an enigmatic smile. "Blind faith can get you into a lot of trouble, Anna."

So many things in San Miguel could get her in a lot of trouble, she thought worriedly. It seemed to be a town simmering with secrets.

"Look," Ben said. "I still have some contacts in the Department of Public Safety. If it'll make you feel any better, I'll give one of them a call and request that the highway patrol be on the look-out for Emily's car. Maybe I'll even take a drive to San Antonio myself, see if I can spot her car along the roadside. It's possible she could have run into trouble coming back last night."

"That's a good idea. I'll go with you." Anna rose quickly from the bench. "I think we should go right now."

Ben stood, too. "Are you sure? You look pretty beat. Why don't you stay and try to get some rest? I'll call you if I find out anything."

But Anna's tone was firm. "I wouldn't be able to rest. Besides, I'm a lot stronger than I look."

Something glinted in Ben's eyes. "Yeah. I kind of got that impression the other night."

ANNA STUDIED Ben's profile as they sped along the highway in his Jeep. He'd been so quiet since they left the hotel, she couldn't help but wonder what he was thinking. Was he annoyed that she'd dragged him out on what he probably considered a wild-goose chase?

But Anna didn't think that was the reason for his silence. He wasn't just preoccupied. He seemed worried about something. Was he still concerned about the shadow Anna had seen on the balcony?

Anna was starting to get a little nervous about that, as well. Ever since Mendoza had suggested the intruder might have been looking for her room, she couldn't shake the uneasy notion that the shadow on her balcony and the break-in might have something to do with her real reason for being in San Miguel.

She still didn't know who was behind the phone calls she'd received in Houston, or what the caller's intent had been. Someone who'd been close to Katherine and now desired contact with Anna?

She shivered as her thoughts drifted back to the day Dr. English had been murdered and she had had the ugly confrontation with Hays on the street. He'd called her a freak, a modern-day Frankenstein. He'd wanted to get under her skin that day, wanted to hurt her the way he perceived she'd hurt him. Was he responsible for the phone calls?

Ben pulled to the shoulder of the road, and Anna glanced around at the primitive landscape. The river was to their right, but a dense thicket—almost as lush as a mangrove—of trees, palmettos and wild honeysuckle made it all but invisible.

"Why are we stopping here?"

"That dirt road we just passed leads down to a boat ramp. I thought I saw a car down there."

He reversed several yards along the shoulder, and then putting the Jeep into first gear, pulled onto the dirt road. As they drove out of the dense shade of the woods into a patch of sunlight, Anna saw the river. And she almost immediately spotted Emily's Volkswagen.

"That's it! That's her car!" She released her seat belt as soon as the Jeep had bumped to a stop.

Ben got out with her. "Wait a minute," he said when she started toward the car. He approached the vehicle more cautiously, squatting every so often to examine the road. "I don't see any other tracks. Doesn't look like anyone drove down here since Emily's car was left here."

"How long ago was that, do you suppose?"

He shrugged. "The tracks look pretty fresh. We know they had to have been made after you saw her yesterday." He walked over to the car and tried the door, then peered in through the window. "Whoever left the car here took the keys and locked the doors."

He moved to the front of the vehicle, examined the ground, then kneeling, motioned for Anna to join him.

"What is it?" she asked, trying to balance on the backs of her heels the way he was. Ben made it look too easy.

He pointed to the ground. "Footprints leading down to the water. Whoever it was wore athletic shoes, but not a brand I recognize. And by the size of the prints and the depth of the impressions, I'd say they were made by a woman."

"Emily was wearing sneakers when she left yesterday," Anna said. "I know because she dropped me off at the garage just before she left for San Antonio."

"One set of prints leading down to the water," Ben

mused. "Makes you wonder if she got into a boat with someone."

Anna frowned as she stared at the footprints. "Why would she do that? Unless she was forced…"

Ben shook his head. "Doesn't look that way. Only one set of prints, no other tire tracks, no sign of a struggle. She even took the time to take her keys and lock her car. I'd say it's more likely she drove down here to meet someone."

"But that doesn't make any sense. When she left the garage, she said she was headed straight for San Antonio."

"Maybe she had a change of plans. Someone could have called her on her cell phone and asked her to meet them here."

"Or lured her here. Think about it, Ben. Emily is determined to prove Katherine was murdered. What if someone called her yesterday and told her they had the proof she's been looking for? I think it's pretty likely she would have gone off with them, especially if it was someone she trusted."

Ben took out his cell phone. "We can speculate about this all day, but, like it or not, we'd better get Mendoza out here."

As Ben made the call, Anna turned to study the river. A dark premonition descended over her. Even if Emily had left with someone of her own free will, Anna had a bad feeling she wouldn't be returning in the same way.

A LITTLE WHILE LATER, Ben dropped Anna in front of the hotel. "Try to get some rest, okay? I'll call if I hear anything."

"You have my cell phone number?" Anna asked.

He patted his shirt pocket. "Right here."

She nodded. "Okay. I guess I'll just wait to hear from you then."

He took her hand before she could slide out of the Jeep, and Anna turned. As their gazes met, a deep awareness settled around her. That strange, disconcerting sensation of having known him before, intimately.

He said nothing, and after a moment, he released her hand, and Anna climbed from the Jeep and hurried into the hotel.

Chapter Eleven

When Anna awakened, she could tell by the shadows in her room that it was late in the day. She'd fallen asleep sometime after Ben dropped her off at the hotel, and had napped for hours, her body demanding the rest it had been deprived of the night before.

Still groggy from such a deep sleep, she dragged herself out of bed and padded across the floor to open the French doors and step out onto the balcony. The sun was just setting over the river, tinting the water with a warm, burnished glow. Anna's gaze went automatically to the ruins of the old mission, and she watched for a moment, thinking she might see again whoever had been in there her first evening at the hotel.

But nothing stirred. Even the mild breeze she'd noticed earlier seemed to have died away, creating an uncanny calm before the approaching twilight.

Anna turned to go back inside, but a sound caught her attention, and she remained motionless for a moment, listening. Someone was playing the piano downstairs.

Even in such breathless tranquility, the faint tinkle

of the piano keys was barely discernible. But Anna knew the tune that was being played.

Heart and Soul.

The hair on the back of her neck lifted as she stood listening to the music. Then rushing back inside, she hurried across the room to the hallway.

She paused outside her door to glance up and down the corridor. No one was about. Emily was still missing and Dwight Gump, the long-term resident of the hotel, was still presumably out of town. That only left Anna and the new guest, Mr. Carter, in Room 203.

As she approached the stairs, she could see that the door to his room was closed, but whether he was inside or not, she had no idea. She had no idea what he looked like, either, or if there even really was a Mr. Carter.

Now you're sounding paranoid, a tiny voice taunted her.

But paranoid or not, there was something strange about Margarete and Acacia Cortina. There was something strange about this hotel, and Anna now had a hard time believing she'd once thought it quaint.

She had a sudden image of Margarete, butcher knife in hand, chasing the hapless felines through the halls of the hotel. And then of Acacia, vampire-like, luring them to their demise.

You really are losing it, Anna told herself as she hurried down the stairs. At the bottom, she bypassed the dining room where the tables were already starting to fill up with the dinner crowd and crept down the hallway that, according to Emily, led to the Cortinas' private quarters. Anna didn't feel comfortable trespassing so brazenly, but she wanted to make sure it really was one of Acacia's students who was playing the piano.

The sound grew louder as she moved down the hallway, but as she neared the door at the end, the playing stopped. Anna pushed open the door, not certain what excuse she would give to Acacia for bursting in on her lesson.

But the room was empty.

Anna stood gazing around. Where had the music come from if not from this room?

The space must once have been a library. Floor-to-ceiling shelves lined three walls, but most of the books were gone. Only a few scattered volumes remained, and Anna wondered if perhaps Margarete had done away with the books when she'd gotten rid of the cats.

A shiver ran up Anna's spine as she entered the room. She experienced a deep uneasiness, but it wasn't the same feeling she'd had in the mission or standing outside Emily's door. On those occasions, she'd been certain she was standing in the presence of evil, or where evil had been. This was more subtle. More…cunning somehow.

An old baby grand piano sat in front of a row of French doors that looked out on the back lawn and the river beyond. One of the doors stood slightly ajar, as if someone had just slipped away. Suppressing another shudder, Anna walked across the room and stepped out onto a stone patio. Her room was directly above the music room which would explain how she'd been able to hear the piano.

But...if Acacia had been giving a lesson only moments earlier, where was she now? Where was her student? Why had they left so suddenly?

As Anna glanced toward the river, she saw a silhouette at the top of the steps that led down to the dock. Just a glimpse, nothing more, but for a moment, she thought it might be Emily.

Leaving the patio, Anna hurried across the lawn to stand at the top of the steps. She couldn't see anyone. Not on the dock or along the bank. Whoever had been there a moment ago had vanished.

The sun had dipped below the horizon by now, and though it was still daylight, the cypress trees that lined the bank cast deep shadows across the water. Fruit bats darted low through the woods, and Anna shivered in the warm twilight. Without the sun, an eerie quality descended over the river. A dark, waiting stillness.

A boat tied up at the dock stirred in the sluggish current, reminding Anna of Ben's speculation earlier that Emily had left her car and gone off willingly in a boat. Had she come back to the hotel in a boat?

A twig snapped behind her, and Anna whirled, startled, then she let out a breath of relief. A middle-aged couple nodded politely and smiled. "Nice evening for a walk," the man murmured as they moved past her to the steps.

Anna waited until they were almost to the bottom, then she followed them down. They turned left along the river and were soon lost to her sight. Anna walked over to the dock and strode to the end where the boat was tied up.

It was a small, fiberglass fishing boat, hardly more than a dinghy, with planks on the inside for seating and a small outboard motor. As Anna peered over the railing, she saw dark stains across the side and in the bottom.

She knelt on the dock, trying to get a better look. With one hand holding on to the railing for support, she leaned as far down as she possibly could.

Blood was smeared over the sides and in the bottom where something—or someone—had been dragged inside.

Anna recoiled in horror. Her first thought was to run to a phone and call Ben. But before she could get to her feet, she heard the wooden planks of the dock creak behind her.

Still kneeling and leaning over the water, she was completely vulnerable to the presence that had crept up behind her.

BEN CLOSED THE FOLDER he'd been reading and rubbed the bridge of his nose. One of his H.P.D. contacts had faxed him the crime scene and lab reports in the Michael English case, and he'd been going over the file all afternoon.

So far, nothing he'd read even remotely tied English's murder to Scorpio. For one thing, Scorpio's other victims—the ones who'd been found, at least—had all been female caucasians. Like those victims, English had been shot in the head, but the slug didn't match any of the bullets taken from the young women. Nor had a scorpion, the killer's signature, been left at the crime scene. The only similarity was the mutilation to the chest cavity. The killer had attempted to cut out the doctor's heart.

But even there, the inconsistencies were glaring. In Scorpio's early kills, the incisions had been crude and brutal, but in the later victims, the mutilation had been accomplished much more cleanly and efficiently.

So why had Michel English's murderer left before the mission was complete? Why leave the heart?

It was possible the killer had run out of time. The murder had taken place in daylight. The killer might well have been frightened off by a barking dog or a passing car.

It was also possible that this was the killer's first attempt at mutilation. A new killer—one less accomplished than Scorpio—could be on the prowl in Houston.

For a moment, Ben considered calling Doug Jamison, the FBI profiler who'd worked on Operation Exterminate, and getting his take on the case. But it was too early for that.

For now, all Ben could do was wait.

And while he waited, the killer could already be stalking the next victim.

Rising from his desk, Ben stretched, then paced to the window to stare out. It was still light out, but the shadows crawling across the shrubbery and topiaries gave the grounds the look of a necropolis.

Restless, Ben decided to take a walk. He strode out of the room and down the hallway, and when he passed Gabby's room, he considered for a moment asking her to join him. But she was probably on her computer and wouldn't want to be interrupted. Besides, Ben really needed to be alone. He needed time to think, to sort through the case.

But a few minutes later, when he found himself on the trail along the river, he knew—had known all along—what his final destination would be.

He was going to see Anna.

He couldn't stop thinking about her, couldn't stop wanting her. In the short time she'd been in San Miguel, she'd gotten under his skin in a big way, and Ben didn't know what in the hell to do about it. Why didn't she just go back to Houston and leave him in peace?

But if she went back to Houston, Ben wondered if he would be far behind her. Ever since he'd heard about the English case, he'd been thinking that it might be time for him to return to the city. Maybe he was wrong about San Miguel. Maybe his prey was still in Houston.

Gabby could go with him if she wanted to. He'd find a way to appease Gwen. They could find a condo or townhouse near a good school. Money was no object, thanks to Katherine.

But the thought of spending her money left a bad taste in Ben's mouth. Besides, he had his pension and a pretty nice nest egg from the book. And he wasn't exactly without prospects.

One of his old partners was now part owner in a private investigation firm in Houston. Ted McElroy had been trying to get Ben to come to work at BMI for years now. The last time Ben had been in Houston—the day Michael English had been murdered—he'd dropped by the BMI offices and Ted had extended the offer again. Ben had never considered it seriously before because deep down he'd harbored the hope that somehow, some way he could get back on the force.

But that was never going to happen. Maybe it was time he accepted the fact that his cops days were over and began to seriously consider Ted's offer.

Someone hurried along the trail toward him, and Ben moved over to allow her to pass. When she drew near, he saw that it was Gwen. The blue jean cutoffs and bikini top she wore were soaking, as was her hair.

"What happened to you?" he asked. "Fall in the river?"

Her eyes glinted with amusement as she stared up at him. "I've just come from a swim. The water's great this time of day."

He frowned. "You shouldn't go swimming alone. The currents look slow but they can be tricky if you aren't careful."

She gave a low laugh as she wrung out her hair. "That's what makes it so much fun."

Ben stared at her for a moment. What she'd just said…the *way* she said it…

She'd never reminded him more of Katherine.

She gave her wet hair a shake. "What's the matter, Ben? You look as if you just saw a ghost."

"Maybe I did," he muttered. "For a moment there—"

"What?"

He paused. "You sounded just like Katherine."

Something flashed in her eyes, an emotion he couldn't quite define. She shook her head again. "I may sound like my sister, but I'm not her. I'm younger than she was, in case you haven't noticed. And stronger. Some might even say prettier."

When Ben said nothing, she smiled coyly. "What's the matter, Ben? Cat got your tongue? Oh, but that's not possible around here, is it? Not since Margarete did away with all the little kitties."

Ben frowned at her tone.

Gwen saw his reaction and laughed. "You know what I think? I think those cats never left the hotel. They're all buried on the grounds somewhere. I wonder if Margarete hears them crying at night?"

"That's a pretty gruesome theory," Ben said.

Gwen laughed again, enjoying herself. "Or maybe it was Acacia. She's always been a little bloodthirsty, and besides, she's told that reincarnated Mayan princess story so many times, I think she's starting to believe it. Maybe she *sacrificed* the cats."

"I thought the Mayans were peaceful," Ben said.

"A common misconception," Gwen said. "They used human sacrifices, too. Cut the hearts out and offered them to the gods just like the Aztecs did. They just didn't enjoy it as much." Her eyes gleamed in the twilight.

"How do you know so much about the Mayans?"

"Katherine told me. She was fascinated by primitive cultures. Where do you think Acacia got the idea that she was a reincarnated Mayan princess? She believed every word Katherine told her, but then..." Gwen paused. "Katherine could make people believe a lot of things, couldn't she, Ben?"

WATER LAPPED against Anna's face, a bracing chill that brought her instantly awake. She was in a boat. She could feel it rocking gently back and forth.

She strained to remember what had happened. Had she fallen off the dock into the boat?

Still slightly dazed, she glanced around, noticing that the seats had been removed. She was lying flat on her back in the bottom of the boat in several inches of water. And then, when she tried to sit up, she discovered that her wrists and ankles were bound with cord and strapped to the oar hooks.

A cold, mind-numbing panic seized her, and Anna began to tug furiously at the bindings. But the harder she pulled, the tighter the knots became until the pain in her wrists and ankles grew agonizing.

Every time she moved, water splashed in her nose and mouth, causing her to sputter, and frantically she lifted her head as high as she could. The water level in the boat was continuing to rise. In another few moments, it would be completely submerged.

Struggling to keep her face above water, Anna cast about frantically for help, but she could barely see over the side of the boat. She called out, hoping, praying that someone from the hotel would hear her.

But as her eyes became accustomed to the deepening twilight, she realized the boat was no longer moored at the dock but anchored half a mile downstream. She could see the ruins of Mission San Miguel rising eerily from the shadows on the bank.

That she had been brought here to this precise spot was no accident. Anna was certain of that. Whoever had done this to her knew the river well. They'd picked the deepest point to send her to her death.

Send her to her death…

Who wanted to kill her? And why?

The same person who'd killed Katherine? Emily?

The questions raged inside Anna's mind, but were gone in an instant, replaced by the more pressing terror of trying to keep her head out of the rising water.

She had to get out of that boat, Anna thought desperately. There were houses along the river. Maybe someone would see her.

But the hope flitted away almost immediately. From the bank, the boat would appear empty. Even if someone took the time to investigate, it would be too late. The craft was already listing badly to one side.

And then, as the water gushed over the edge, the boat flipped, leaving the bottom momentarily exposed on the surface while Anna was trapped underneath.

The cold river water took her breath away, but for a moment, the weightlessness of her body made her feel as if she were free. Then the boat began to sink, carrying her with it, and Anna redoubled her efforts to free herself, straining and tugging at her bindings until one hand finally came loose.

She tore at the other cord, knowing there was precious little time. Once the boat settled on the bottom, she would be trapped forever. No one would ever know what happened to her...

Her lungs were screaming for air, but miraculously, the bindings on her wrist suddenly slipped away. Anna saw a dark figure in front of her and realized that someone was in the water with her. Her ankles came free next, and then she was being pulled from beneath the sinking boat.

As soon as her head broke the surface of the water, Anna drew in long gulps of air. Sputtering and coughing, she tried to tread water, but her legs and arms were too weak. She was sinking again.

Then suddenly, Ben was beside her, wrapping a strong arm around her, instructing her in a calm, authoritative voice to relax and not to struggle.

With an effort, Anna did as she was told, but it wasn't easy. Adrenaline still raged through her bloodstream, and her instinct for survival, always powerful, demanded that she fight. Putting her life in Ben's hands without a struggle took a monumental effort on her part.

Luckily, he was a strong swimmer. He had them to safety in a matter of seconds. They both collapsed on the sandy bank, Anna on her hands and knees, coughing up water.

Ben said a little breathlessly, "We need to get you to a hospital."

"No," she protested weakly. "I'm fine."

"You almost drowned, Anna. We have to get you checked out." He lifted her into his arms, and then rose easily with her weight.

Anna was too shaky to fight him. "I'll be fine," she said on a trembling breath. "I swallowed some water, but other than that, I think I'm okay."

"We'll let a doctor decide that."

She buried her face in Ben's chest, letting the steady beat of his heart calm her until, several minutes later, he carried her into the house.

Katherine's house.

Something happened to Anna then. Something she couldn't explain. She'd almost died at the bottom of the river, and she should be grateful to be inside the comforting warmth of a home. Any home. But there was something about this house...

The first time she'd seen it, she'd thought the place held secrets. She still thought that. But she no longer wanted to unveil them.

As if sensing her uneasiness, Ben's arms tightened around her. They were standing in the foyer, dripping water all over some exotic rug, but he seemed oblivious to the damage. "You're still shivering," he murmured. "I'll just get the car and we'll drive to the hospital."

As foreboding a place as this house now seemed, the mention of the hospital alerted Anna to a new danger. An examination would reveal the scar on her chest, and the doctor on call would undoubtedly insist on knowing her medical history. If she told him about the transplant...if Ben found out...

He's bound to find out sooner or later, a little voice warned.

Not that way, Anna thought. She needed time to explain to him exactly why she'd decided to carry out such a deception. She had to somehow find a way to make him understand.

She pushed herself away from him. "Please put me down. I'm fine. I don't need a doctor."

He scowled in disapproval. "A near drowning is

nothing to take lightly, Anna. We need to make sure your lungs weren't damaged—''

"But I was only under water for a few seconds. Less than a minute, surely. It seemed like an eternity, but it wasn't. I never lost consciousness. I'm fine, Ben. Really.''

He gave her an exasperated look. "Why not let a doctor make that determination?''

"Because I spent a good portion of the last two years of my life in hospitals," she blurted. "I don't want to go back to one unless it's absolutely necessary.''

He stared at her for a moment, then shrugged. "Okay, if that's the way you want it. You're a grown woman. I can't make you go.''

"Thank you.''

"But we have to call the police," Ben said. "Someone tried to kill you. You weren't tied to that boat by accident.''

"I know, but it's already starting to seem like a bad dream, like it happened to someone else.'' She shuddered and Ben wrapped an arm around her shoulders.

"Come in here," he said, leading her into the living room. "Sit down and I'll get you a blanket.''

"But I'm all wet," Anna protested. "It'll ruin the sofa.''

"Who the hell cares about that?" Ben turned abruptly and left the room. He was only gone for a few minutes, but delayed shock was already taking a toll on Anna's nerves by the time he came back.

She trembled uncontrollably as he wrapped a blanket around her shoulders and tucked it snuggly around her legs. "Still think you don't need a doctor? You're shaking so badly I can almost hear your teeth chatter."

"I—I'm o-okay." She clutched the blanket tightly to her chest.

"Are you up to talking? Can you tell me what happened?"

"I'm not sure I know." She put a hand to the back of her head, finding the knot. The wound was tender to the touch, but surprisingly, it didn't hurt. "Someone must have knocked me out," she murmured.

"Where?"

"Back at the hotel." She took a moment to test her memory. "I heard someone playing the piano so I went down to the music room, but no one was there. I saw someone on the steps, and I thought it might be Emily. Or Acacia."

Ben stared at her with a puzzled frown. "So you followed them? I can understand if you thought it was Emily, but why would you follow Acacia?"

Because I wanted to ask her if she was the one who's been playing "Heart and Soul". Aloud Anna said, "I don't know. I guess it was just a spur of the moment thing." That much was true at least. "I saw the boat tied to the dock and I remembered how you said that Emily may have gotten into a boat of her own free will. I thought maybe she'd come back to the hotel. So I went to check it out, and I saw bloodstains. I think someone must have come up behind me then, hit me and pushed me into the boat. The next thing I knew, I woke up strapped to the oar hooks and the boat was sinking." She glanced at Ben. "You saved my life."

He shrugged off her gratitude. "I'm just glad I came along when I did."

"Why were you out here?" she asked suddenly. "At just the right moment?"

Something flickered in his eyes. "That's not an accusation, I hope."

"No, of course not. But you have to admit the coincidence is pretty amazing."

"Maybe it wasn't such a coincidence."

Anna frowned. "What do you mean?"

Ben looked suddenly at a loss. He rose and walked over to the windows to stare out. "As it happens, I was on my way to the hotel to see you."

"You...were?"

He glanced over his shoulder, meeting her gaze. "I can't seem to stay away from you."

The admission stunned her, although Anna wasn't sure why. She felt the same way, had from the moment she'd first laid eyes on him.

But things had changed between them now. She could sense it. Ben had risked his life to save her, and Anna knew if the situation were reversed, she would have done the same for him. The bond between them was no longer merely a physical attraction, if it had ever been only that. The connection now was deeper, more spiritual and much more complex.

Love at first sight? Anna wasn't convinced she believed in the concept still, but whatever she and Ben had, it wasn't going away. Not in a day. Not in a year. Maybe not ever.

He came back to the sofa and sat down beside her. "When I got to the mission tonight, I stopped for some reason to stare at the river. I saw something in the water. I started to ignore it, but something warned me not to. When I swam out to it, I saw that it was the bottom of a boat, and I somehow knew you were down there, in danger. I don't know how I knew. It was the oddest thing, Anna. I rarely carry a pocket knife, but I had one with me tonight."

To cut away the cords.

Electricity tingled along Anna's nerve endings, making her shiver.

Ben saw her and reached over to tug the blanket more securely around her. "You're still shaking. You need to get out of those wet clothes while I call the police. Come on," he said, pulling her to her feet. "A hot shower will do you a world of good. I'll have Gwen find something for you to put on. No argument, okay?"

She shook her head. "No argument. But Ben—" When he turned to glance down at her, she paused. "Everything you just told me…knowing that I was in danger…the pocketknife. How do you explain it?"

"I can't," he said with a shrug. "I guess we'll just have to chalk it up to luck."

But it was something more than luck, and they both knew it.

Chapter Twelve

Anna knew immediately that the room Ben showed her to was his own. The heavy furniture and dark accessories were very masculine, but with a hint of the same elegance she'd seen in the rest of the house.

As she stood gazing around, Ben said with some irony, "This room is as big as my entire apartment back in Houston."

"It's beautiful," Anna murmured. "The whole house is incredible."

"Incredibly creepy," he muttered.

She turned in surprise. "You feel it, too, then. I thought it was just me."

He frowned. "I've never liked this house."

"I know it sounds crazy, but when I first saw it, I thought it had a secretive quality."

Ben's expression turned grim. "It's not crazy. This house does have secrets."

Anna shivered as she stared up at him. "And you know what they are, don't you?"

He hesitated. "Not all of them."

"The first time I saw you, I thought you had secrets, too," Anna said softly.

"Don't we all?" He turned then and walked across the room to open a door. Reaching inside, he turned on the bathroom light. "There're plenty of fresh towels, soap, shampoo, everything you need."

He watched her from the bathroom doorway, and Anna suddenly grew very nervous. There was something so darkly sensuous about the way he looked, something so dangerously seductive about the way he looked at her.

When she walked across the room to join him, he moved back, allowing her to enter the stone-and-marble bathroom, done in monochromatic shades of beige.

"I'll give you some privacy," he murmured, then closed the door between them.

Anna gazed around again, hesitant for some reason to undress in Ben's bathroom. Then telling herself she was being ridiculous, she turned on the shower and let the water get hot while she quickly stripped off her clothes. Stepping into the steamy shower, she closed her eyes for a moment, reveling in the instant warmth that invaded her. The river had been so cold....

She stayed in the shower for a long time, then as the water began to cool, she reluctantly turned off the taps and stepped out. Drying off quickly, she wrapped one beige towel around her body and wound another around her hair.

As she cleared the steam from the mirror, Anna's gaze went immediately to the thick, ropey scar that split her chest cavity in two.

What man would want to see that in bed?

Unbidden, Hays's words came back to her, and she remembered something else, too—the dream she'd had her first night in San Miguel. Ben had been making love to her, but when he'd seen her scar, he'd vanished into thin air.

She suddenly wondered if that dream could have been a portent, and with that thought, Anna abruptly turned away from the mirror. Opening the bathroom door a crack, she glanced into the bedroom. Finding the room empty, she walked out, her gaze going straight to the bed where a red dress had been laid out on top of the spread.

Anna walked over and picked up the garment, holding it against her body. It was a simple sheath in a beautiful semi-sheer silk. The fabric gleamed against her pale skin, and she knew when she put it on, it would mold itself to even her meager curves.

Anna had only met Gwen Draven once, but she couldn't picture her in such a garment. The dress seemed more suited to…

Katherine.

This was exactly the kind of dress Katherine would have worn.

Was that why she was so drawn to it? Anna wondered. The color. The fabric. Everything about it was perfection. Everything about it screamed seduction….

Anna had a closetful of expensive garments at home—designer suits, cocktail dresses, casual slacks and sweaters—all in somber colors.

She'd never owned a red dress in her life. Red wasn't even her color, she told herself, as she slipped it over her head. The fabric glided like a breath of warm air over her hips.

On bare feet, Anna walked across the room to the full-length mirror and preened in front of it.

Amazing.

The dress not only made her feel different, but she also looked different. A warm rosy glow replaced her usual pale complexion, and her damp hair hung in heavy waves down her back. Even her body looked different. She'd been very thin since the surgery and her restrictive diet, but the dress made her look as if she had curves. Feminine curves. Womanly curves.

She ran her hands down her sides, admiring the cut and drape of the garment, the sensuality of the silk. Her gaze lifted suddenly, and she saw Ben in the doorway watching her.

His arms were folded as he leaned one shoulder against the frame. His gaze met hers in the mirror, and an electric shock rode up Anna's spine. Then, very slowly, he moved toward her.

Anna didn't turn as he approached, but instead she watched him in the mirror. When he stood behind her, he lifted his hands to her shoulders. "My God," he breathed. "You look…incredible."

"It's the dress," Anna murmured.

"It's not the dress." His voice had gone all deep and husky. His fingers feathered down her arms to entangle briefly with hers. Then, with slow deliberation, he moved his hands to her hips, sliding them slowly up her sides, tracing her waist, grazing her breasts. He put an arm around her waist and drew her to him.

Anna leaned into him, letting her head tip back as he bent to nuzzle her neck, to whisper in her ear what he wanted to do to her.

She couldn't believe they were having such an intimate moment. They were both still dressed, but she'd never been so aroused in her life. Never wanted a man as badly as she wanted Ben at that moment.

It didn't matter that they were strangers. He didn't seem like a stranger at all to Anna.

It didn't matter that only a little while ago, she'd been fighting for her life beneath a cold, dark river. Ben had saved her.

With a sigh, Anna turned her head and his mouth found hers. He greedily parted her lips and then plunged his tongue inside to tangle with hers. She met his thrusts and matched them with her own fevered urgency, moaning softly as he lifted his hand to her breast.

When he broke the kiss, Anna buried her face in his neck, drinking in the scent of him, the feel of him, the very essence of him. Then she turned slightly so that she could see their reflections in the mirror. So that she could watch his hands glide over her, stroking her, making her want him even more.

A slight movement in the mirror drew her gaze away from Ben, and Anna saw that someone else watched them from the doorway. She had only a brief glimpse before the figure turned and darted away.

Anna stiffened. "Someone was in the doorway, watching us."

Ben lifted his head. He had the dazed look of a drunk. "What?" he said thickly.

"Someone was in the doorway. I think it might have been Gabby." Anna turned in his arms. "Oh, Ben...she saw us...."

"It's okay. We were just kissing."

But it wasn't exactly as innocent as all that, either. Anna had been very close to succumbing to the passion, to the almost unbearable sexual tension that had been building inside her from the moment she'd entered this house.

"You'd better go after her," she said. "She may be upset."

Ben ran a hand through his dark hair. "You're probably right. I'll go talk to her." He strode across the room and turned at the door. "The police are on the way. You can wait downstairs if you want to."

And then he was gone. Anna hugged her arms tightly to her middle, telling herself that it was only her imagination that the room had suddenly grown quite cold.

But no longer comfortable in Ben's bedroom, she stepped into the hallway. She'd meant to go downstairs and wait for the police as Ben had suggested, but her gaze was drawn to an open door across the hallway. As Anna moved past it, she glanced inside.

A lamp had been left on, and the opulence of the room drew her inside. The walls were chartreuse glazed with gold, and the draperies were a fine Indian silk trimmed with crystal beads. The huge four-poster bed was adorned with a plush cheetah throw and stacked high with pillows in delicate embroidered silks.

A painting of a woman hung over the bed. She was

dressed in a beautiful red gown that glowed like a ruby in the subtle lighting.

It was a life-size portrait of Katherine, but the artist's brushstrokes were so clever and subtle that Anna could almost believe for a moment it was Katherine's ghost hovering over her. Those dark, knowing eyes seemed alive somehow, and the sly, sensuous smile taunted Anna.

Across from the portrait, French doors opened onto a balcony, and Anna moved across the room to glance out. A curving stone staircase led down into a walled courtyard where a lighted fountain trickled in the center. In the cast-off illumination, Anna saw a young girl hiding in the shadows. It had to be Gabby.

Anna watched her for a moment, then opened the door and stepped out onto the balcony. She was almost at the bottom of the stairs before Gabby heard her footsteps—or sensed her presence—and whirled. In the glow from the fountain, her skin looked very pale. Paler, even, than Anna's.

She said on a gasp, "Mother?"

Anna was at once stricken with guilt. "Oh, Gabby, no. I'm sorry. My name is Anna Sebastian. I'm...a friend of Ben's."

"I thought you were my mother's friend," the girl said coldly. She sat down on a nearby bench, her gaze still on Anna.

"I wasn't actually friends with your mother," Anna said carefully.

"Then why are you wearing her dress?"

Anna glanced down. "I had an accident earlier.

I…fell in the river. Ben asked Gwen to find me something to wear."

"And she picked out that dress?"

"Yes. I'm sorry if I've upset you," Anna said softly. "I'll change if you'd like."

Gabby shrugged. "No, I guess it's okay."

"Are you sure you don't mind?"

She shrugged again, then turned to stare at the fountain.

Anna studied her for a moment in the dim light. She was a plain girl by most standards, but Anna thought she had a very interesting face. Her cheekbones were high and angular, her eyes wide-set and dark, radiating, even from a distance, a cool, keen intelligence. Her lips were full and lush like her mother's, and in time, on an older face, they would probably become very seductive.

She turned suddenly. "I know what you're thinking. It's what people always think."

"What's that?"

"I don't look anything like my mother."

"I wouldn't say that." Anna tilted her head. "There's a definite resemblance, but you have your own unique look. And you have the kind of face that will become even more striking as you grow older."

Gabby rolled her eyes. "That's what people say when they can't think of anything good to say. Besides." She gave Anna a cool appraisal. "You don't have to be nice to me. I already know why you're here."

Anna's breath quickened. "What do you mean?"

Gabby lifted her chin. "I know why you came to

San Miguel.'' She withdrew a piece of paper from a pocket in her dress. "Here. I think this belongs to you.''

Anna walked over and took the paper from Gabby. She sat down on the bench and unfolded it. The moment she saw the contents, her stomach churned with dread.

It was the anonymous letter she'd written to her donor's family. The letter she'd never gotten a response to.

Anna lifted her gaze. "Where did you get this?''

Gabby shrugged. "It came in the mail.''

Anna found it very difficult to keep her cool. She stared down at the letter, but the words blurred suddenly. She couldn't make them out, but it didn't matter. She knew that letter by heart. She'd agonized over it for days. "Did anyone else see it? Ben or Gwen?''

Gabby shook her head. She took the letter from Anna's trembling fingers and returned it to her pocket.

"Why didn't you show it to them?''

Gabby shrugged again. "Because they would have just thrown it away. They wouldn't have wanted to find you.''

"But you did?''

The girl turned to stare at the fountain. "Why wouldn't I want to find you. You have my mother's heart.''

Tears stung Anna's eyes, and for a moment, the urge to reach out to the unhappy child beside her was almost unbearable. She knew what it was like to be lonely. She knew what it was like to miss a mother's comforting arms.

"If you wanted to meet me, why didn't you write to the hospital?" Anna finally asked.

"Because they still wouldn't have told me who you were. They wouldn't have released any kind of information to a kid. So I figured out another way to get in touch with you."

"How?"

When she didn't respond, Anna said anxiously, "Gabby, did you know my identity before I came here?"

"I figured it out by accident. I saw an article about you on the Internet. It was from a Houston paper. The reporter was writing about a trial you'd been involved in, and he said you'd gotten a heart transplant. He even mentioned the date. It was the same day my mother died so I knew you had to be the one. I put your name in a search engine and found out a lot of other stuff about you."

Which was exactly what Anna had done with Katherine's name. Only, it was a little disconcerting to find the shoe on the other foot. She couldn't help but feel that her privacy had been violated, but wasn't that exactly what she'd done to Ben and Gabby and Gwen by coming here in the first place?

The girl got up and walked over to the fountain, trailing her fingers in the cool, clear water.

Anna got up, too. "Did you call my apartment in Houston and play the piano over the phone? That tune I've heard you play here. 'Heart and Soul.'"

Gabby shrugged. "I don't know what you're talking about."

"Are you sure?"

"My mother played the piano beautifully," Gabby said, ignoring Anna's question. "She could have been a concert pianist if she'd wanted to. Did you know that?"

"From what I've learned about your mother, she had a great many talents."

"Oh, she did. You have no idea."

"Gabby, about those phone calls—"

She turned suddenly. "Did you tell Ben that you have my mother's heart?"

The question sent a tremor along Anna's nerve endings. "No. Not yet."

"Why not?"

"Because—"

"Because you're afraid he'll hate you when he finds out, aren't you?"

"No, of course not—"

"He hated her, you know. My mother. He despised her. He wanted her dead."

"I don't believe that."

"It's true." Gabby turned back to the fountain. "And he'll want you dead, too, when he finds out."

GABBY'S WARNING rang in Anna's head all through the interview with Mendoza. She could hardly meet Ben's gaze, and once she'd given her statement, she suddenly couldn't wait to leave that house. Katherine's house.

Mendoza stood, returning his notebook and pen to the back pocket of his jeans. "Can I give you a lift back to your hotel, Ms. Sebastian?"

Anna opened her mouth to answer, but before she

could utter a word, Ben said, "I'll take her back when she's ready to go." He turned to Anna. "But I really think it would be best if you stayed here tonight."

"Here?" He'd caught her completely by surprise.

Ben lifted a brow at her reaction. "Why not? You'll be safe here."

"What makes you think that?" Mendoza cut in.

Ben's gaze darkened. "Because I'll make sure of it."

Anna said reluctantly, "I'm not sure my staying here is such a good idea, Ben."

He frowned. "Why not?" He took her arm and pulled her away from Mendoza. "Anna, what's going on? Why don't you want to stay here tonight?"

"I just don't think it's a good idea," she said stubbornly.

"You're being ridiculous. Someone tried to kill you tonight. Why won't you let me protect you?"

"Because I don't want to stay *here,*" she blurted. "Not in this house. I know that sounds crazy, but I don't feel safe here, Ben. And I don't want to risk upsetting Gabby."

"Gabby?" He gave her an incredulous look. "I don't want to upset her, either, but I'd rather have her a little ticked off than have your life endangered."

He had a point, but Gabby might also blurt out the truth in her anger, and that was a chance Anna didn't want to take.

Mendoza said behind them, "You don't need to worry about her safety, Porter. I'm posting a guard in the lobby of the hotel tonight, and another to patrol the grounds. No one will get in or out without my knowledge. She wouldn't be any safer at Fort Knox.''

Anna turned to Ben. "I think that's for the best," she said softly. "Please don't worry about me. I'll be fine."

"I'm already worried," he said darkly. "But I can't stop you from going."

He walked them to the car, and as they drove away from the house, Mendoza glanced in his rearview mirror. "Porter seems pretty worried about you."

"He was the one who rescued me earlier. He saw firsthand what someone tried to do to me."

Mendoza gave her an assessing glance. "Let me ask you something. Don't you find it a pretty unlikely coincidence that he just happened to be at exactly the right place at the right time to rescue you?"

She turned with a frown. "I hope you don't consider Ben a suspect."

"I consider everyone around you a suspect, Ms. Sebastian. You should, too."

A shiver ran up Anna's spine as she turned to study his profile. "Maybe the person who tried to kill me wasn't someone close to me. Maybe I was just a random target."

"The victim of a psychopath who kills for the sake of killing?" He shot her a glance. "Have you ever heard of a serial killer named Richard Allen Hinkle?"

Anna thought for a moment. "I may have, but I don't recall anything about him. Why?"

"He targeted a certain area of Chicago back in the late seventies, killed half a dozen women or so, all young, pretty, single. It was a sensational case at the time, but now Hinkle's been pretty much forgotten in the wake of the Ted Bundies and the Jeffrey Dahmers.'' He paused. ''Hinkle wrote letters to the police and signed them 'Lady Killer.' The police didn't learn his true identity until much later.

''The cop he singled out in his letters was the lead detective on the case. All during that summer, the cop and the killer carried on this bizarre correspondence. The detective became quite famous. He appeared on news broadcasts, did radio spots, you name it. A book was even written about him.''

Anna had a very uncomfortable feeling about the story. ''What does any of this have to do with what happened to me?''

Mendoza glanced at her. ''Do you have any idea what the detective's name was?''

She shook her head.

''His name was Richard Allen Hinkle.''

''But I thought you said—''

''I did. When the killer was finally caught, he turned out to be none other than the lead detective on the case.''

Anna's hands clenched into fists at her sides. ''You're not suggesting that Ben was responsible for the Scorpio killings, are you?'' When he didn't answer, Anna said angrily, ''But he was wounded himself. Almost killed. He had to quit the police force because of what happened to him. Scorpio took everything from him.''

''Not everything.'' Mendoza scowled at the road. ''Ben Porter made a small fortune from the book he wrote about the killings. And because of that book, he met and married Katherine Sprague. After she died, he became even richer.''

''And now you're suggesting he had something to do with her death, as well?'' Anna glared at him. ''Katherine committed suicide. You headed the investigation yourself.''

''None of the evidence was inconsistent with suicide, that's true,'' Mendoza agreed. ''And it's also true that the latest advancements in forensic science make it almost impossible to fake a suicide and get away with it. But if anyone could pull it off, it would be a cop, right? Or a former cop.''

Emily had said almost the exact same thing to Anna. She, too, had suspected Ben was responsible for Katherine's death. And now Emily was missing.

''Has there been any news of Emily Winsome?'' Anna asked suddenly.

''No. But don't worry. After what happened to you tonight, I'll be taking a closer look at her disappearance.''

He pulled up in front of the hotel and parked. In the light from the dash, his dark eyes looked a little sinister as he turned to Anna. ''If I were you, I'd consider returning to Houston as soon as possible. It's only a few hours' drive. Surely you have someone who could come and pick you up.''

''What makes you think I'd be any safer in Houston?'' she asked.

He studied her for a moment. ''Why do I get the feeling you're holding out on me, Anna?''

''I'm not.''

''Nothing else you need to tell me?''

"What are you getting at, Detective?"

"You came to San Miguel for a reason. Sooner or later, I'll find out what it is. But let's just hope by the time I do, it won't be too late to help you."

Chapter Thirteen

Anna immediately spotted the officer Mendoza had sent to stand guard in the lobby. He was in the sitting room reading a book, but when he heard the front door open, he glanced up. His keen gaze met Anna's and he nodded briefly before returning his attention to his novel.

The murmur of voices from the dining room reminded Anna that she hadn't had anything to eat since lunch. She walked over to the front desk where Acacia stood talking on the phone. When she saw Anna, she hung up quickly and turned with a smile that didn't quite reach her dark eyes. *"Buenas tardes."*

"Good evening," Anna said. "I know room service isn't offered at the hotel, but I was wondering if I could get a sandwich delivered to my room. You can just add the extra cost to my bill."

"I'll see what I can do." Acacia's gaze flitted over Anna, taking in the formfitting red dress. When she looked up, she was no longer smiling. "You've had quite a night, I hear."

Anna said in surprise, "You heard about what happened?"

Acacia shrugged. "This is San Miguel. News travels very quickly. Besides." She nodded to the officer stationed in the next room. "Detective Mendoza didn't have any easy time convincing Mama to allow his men to remain on the premises. I can't say she's too happy about the situation."

Perhaps Margarete should be more concerned about the ease with which one of her guest's rooms had been ransacked, or the fact that that same guest was now missing and Anna had been attacked on the dock behind the hotel.

She said coolly, "I'm very sorry for the inconvenience, but at least we should all be able to get a good night's sleep tonight. If the person who attacked me is still lurking about, he won't be able to get into the hotel. Detective Mendoza has assured me that no one will enter or leave without his knowing about it."

"I suppose that *should* make us feel safer," Acacia agreed with a guileless smile. "Unless, of course, whoever attacked you is already inside the hotel."

AS SOON AS SHE GOT to her room, Anna called Laurel.

"I'm so glad you called," Laurel said. "I've been sitting here debating on whether or not to call you."

"Is something wrong?"

"I don't know. I hope not." She paused. "It's Hays, Anna. He's been by here again."

Anna frowned. "When?"

"The day you left. He insisted on seeing you. When I told him you were out of town, he tried to find out where you'd gone. I didn't tell him anything, naturally, but..."

That "but" made Anna nervous. "But what, Laurel?"

"He asked to use the phone. He said the battery on his cell phone had gone dead, and he needed to contact a client right away. He sounded desperate, Anna, and you know there's always been something about Hays that I find rather pitiful. It's so obvious he's never gotten over you."

Anna wasn't so sure about that. It was true Hays seemed to have a hard time letting go of the past, but she thought he was long past harboring any romantic or sentimental thoughts about their relationship. He'd seemed neither romantic nor sentimental that day she'd seen him outside her apartment. What he'd been was cruel.

"So what is it that has you so worried?" she asked Laurel.

"After he'd gone, I realized that I'd left the name and number of the hotel where you're staying by the phone. He could have seen it and guessed that's where to find you. I thought he might try to get in touch with you there."

"I haven't heard from him," Anna said. "Maybe you've been worrying for nothing."

Laurel sighed in relief. "I hope so. But I thought you should know just the same," she paused. "So when are you coming home, Anna?"

"In a day or two. As soon as my car is ready."

"I could drive down there and pick you up," Laurel offered.

"No, don't do that." The last thing Anna wanted was to drag Laurel into the middle of whatever was going on in San Miguel. She was safe in Houston as long as Anna stayed in San Miguel.

"Are you sure you're okay? You don't sound like yourself, Anna."

"I'm fine. I'm just a little tired tonight. I plan to go to bed early."

"You're taking your medications?"

"Yes. Like clockwork."

"You're eating well and getting plenty of rest?"

Anna sighed. "Yes. All of the above."

They chatted for a few more minutes, then hung up. Anna leaned back against the headboard, and thought about her conversation with Mendoza. She wondered if he was checking into her background. If he found out about her transplant, would he be able to put two and two together the way Gabby had? Would he tell Ben?

Why hadn't Gabby told him? Anna had a feeling the girl was responsible for the phone calls to her apartment, but she had no idea what her motive might be. If she'd wanted contact with the woman who had her mother's heart, why not just say so? Why not try to arrange a meeting? Why play games?

The one thing Anna did know was that the more people who learned about her transplant, the greater the chance that Ben would find out. She had to tell him.

All through the light dinner she'd had brought up to her room, Anna pondered how to do it. Should she just blurt it out? *I've had a heart transplant, Ben, and Katherine was my donor.*

Or should she try for more subtlety? *So how do you feel about organ donations?*

His reaction would probably be the same in either scenario. He would be shocked, and he'd need time to get used to the idea. He might even be angry with her for not telling him sooner.

But Anna hoped once he'd had time to think it through, he'd come to the same conclusion as she. It didn't matter whose heart beat inside her chest. She was still the same person. She was still Anna.

After brushing her teeth, washing her face and taking her evening meds, Anna slipped into a pair of her new pajamas, then climbed into bed. When she finally fell into an exhausted sleep, she dreamed about Ben.

He waited for her in bed. His gaze dark and smoldering, he watched as she slid her blouse slowly off her shoulders and then stepped out of her skirt. By the time she reached the bed, she was naked. As was he.

He reached up to tangle his fingers in her hair, pulling her mouth down to his. When he finally broke the kiss, he was the one this time who traced a finger along her scar.

Even in her dream, Anna's first instinct was to recoil, but she didn't. She let him touch her. For as long as he wanted.

His dark gaze found hers in the darkness. "I know who you are," he said in a deep, husky whisper. "I know why you're here."

As she moved over him, he said in that same dark voice, "You came here to take her place."

Anna shot bolt upright in bed, certain that the

dream had awakened her. Then she realized that the ringing of her cell phone on the nightstand was what had actually dragged her from sleep. Thinking it might be Laurel, she pushed the talk button and lifted it to her ear.

"Laurel?"

"Who's Laurel?"

Anna shivered at the sound of Ben's voice. "My stepmother." She paused. "How did you get my cell phone number?"

"You gave it to me earlier so that I could call if I heard anything about Emily."

Anna shifted back against the pillows. "*Have* you heard something about her?"

"No. The reason I'm calling is because…I've been worried about you, Anna. I had to make sure you were okay."

"I'm fine." She seemed to be saying that a lot lately. Maybe if she said it enough it would be true. "There's really no need for you to worry. Mendoza has an officer in the lobby, and another patrolling the grounds. I saw him out there earlier."

"Yeah, so did I. I saw him when I slipped past him."

Anna frowned into the darkness. "Slipped past him? Where are you?"

"Standing on your balcony."

Anna shot back up in bed and glanced at the window, but she saw nothing. Then suddenly a shadow appeared on the balcony, and she gasped even though she knew it was Ben.

"What are you doing out there?"

"I don't trust Mendoza's men to keep you safe. And with good reason, as it turns out."

"So you came to guard me yourself?" she asked incredulously. "How long have you been out there?"

"Awhile."

"And you're just now letting me know?"

He paused. "I didn't want to wake you, but just now, I thought I heard you cry out."

Anna's cheeks flamed in the darkness. She must have cried out in her sleep while she'd been dreaming about him. "Are you going to stay out there all night?" she murmured.

"Unless you decide to invite me in." His voice deepened, became more intimate. "What do you say, Anna?"

Her stomach tightened with awareness, with anticipation. "Do you really think that's a good idea?"

"It's been coming to this all along. Ever since the moment we first met. You know it as well as I do."

She could see his silhouette through the gauzy curtains at the French doors, and a part of her—a very big part—wanted desperately to let him. To let it happen. He was right. It had been coming to this.

But was it fair to share the most profound intimacy that could exist between a man and a woman when she hadn't yet shared the truth?

"Open the door, Anna," he urged softly.

And God help her, she couldn't resist. She put away the phone and rose on legs that were already trembling in anticipation.

When she opened the door, it was as if all the air suddenly rushed out of it, and she couldn't breathe.

Her skin tingled all over. For the longest moment, they stood with their gazes locked, and then it finally dawned on her that he wouldn't come inside unless he could be very certain she wanted him to.

Reaching for his hand, she silently drew him into her room. She closed and locked the door, then turning, found him standing so close, she almost gasped.

He lifted a hand to touch her hair, and then a second later, she was in his arms and he was kissing her. Kissing her as if he would never stop kissing her. Long, deep, desperate kisses that left them both breathless.

Anna fumbled with the buttons on his shirt, somehow managed to undo them, and then slid the fabric over his shoulders and down his arms. He slung the shirt aside, then helped her with the rest of his clothing. His shoes, socks, jeans, underwear—all discarded in a matter of moments. He strode naked to the bed and lay down, waiting for her.

His body was magnificent. Lean, tanned, muscular. Anna couldn't stop looking at him.

Propping himself on his elbow, he watched her watching him. She knew that his eyes were dark and seductive, the way they had been in her dream.

"Undress for me, Anna." His voice was from her dream, too. Deep and husky. Sexy beyond belief. "Let me watch you."

She did as he asked, unfastening the buttons on her pajama top, then slowly, deliberately sliding the silky fabric down her arms. Her bottoms came next and when she stepped out of them, she heard the sharp intake of his breath.

Had he seen her scar?

No, no, she wouldn't think about that now. She wouldn't let that come between them.

She wouldn't risk letting him slip away from her when she had him so close. When she was about to experience the most profound and thrilling moment of her life.

And it would be. Somehow she knew their love-making would change her forever.

She walked slowly to the bed, anticipating his next move. He knew it well. It was as if he'd had the same dream.

He reached up to weave his fingers through her hair, and then he pulled her toward him for a kiss that drew a gasping shiver from Anna. His hands moved over her, touching her intimately, stroking her, making her burn for him.

Anna was still kneeling on the bed beside him, leaning over him, her hair falling over her shoulders. He drew her on top of him, breaking the kiss to skim his lips across her neck and down her throat. He slid down in bed, finding her breasts and flicking his tongue across them, then he moved lower, his warm breath fanning her stomach. Then lower still...

Anna's fingers curled around the headboard. Her body felt as if it were a wire that had suddenly been pulled too taut. Ben's intimate kisses would surely snap her. But somehow she managed to hold on, even when he put his hands on her hips and pulled her down on him.

It was as if someone else took over her body then. Anna stared down at him as she began to move. Long, slow, deep strokes that drew a low groan from his throat.

He took control then, grasping her hips, increasing the rhythm until Anna knew she couldn't hold on much longer. She'd been so near the edge from their very first kiss, but she didn't want it to end yet. She wanted it to go on forever. The sensations storming through her were so powerful, so dangerously delicious.

But it was too late. She was suddenly in a freefall. She threw her head back in abandon as shudder after shudder racked both their bodies.

After a moment, she fell against Ben, spent, sated and yet somehow still deeply aroused. Maybe it was the exquisite sensuality of the afterglow. Their bodies were still joined, and Ben's arms were around her, holding her so tightly it seemed as if he would never let her go.

Anna buried her face in his neck, and for a while, neither of them said a word. Then finally she lifted her head to stare down at him. He smiled slightly as she cupped his face with her hands and kissed him.

They kissed for the longest time. Slow, languid, completely satisfying kisses until she felt Ben's body begin to respond. Her nerve endings tingled in anticipation as he rolled them over so that now it was he staring down at her.

He took his time with her. Kissing her deeply. Caressing her so intimately, Anna thought she would die from the thrill of it. And all the while, he continued a slow, exquisite rhythm inside her.

The buildup was slower this time, but the explosion, when it finally happened, was no less devastating. No less shattering. They clung to each other for long moments afterward, and then later, they showered together, taking turns underneath the water, lathering each other, and Ben washed her hair with the jasmine-scented shampoo.

Anna forgot about her scar. Or rather, she wouldn't let herself think about it. And Ben pretended not to notice, although he had to. It was no small mark. It was long and thick and deep, a constant reminder of how close she'd come to death.

But for now, she could pretend that she didn't notice it, either. She could pretend that she was still a beautiful, desirable woman whom Ben found utterly irresistible. The look in his eyes made her almost believe it.

They met back in bed. Ben lay on his back, propped against the headboard, and Anna curled against his side, nestled safely in the crook of his arm. She put her hand on his chest, feeling the steady rhythm of his heart.

"Are you going to tell me what happened to you?" he murmured.

Anna closed her eyes. "The scar, you mean."

"Yes. But if you'd rather not talk about it—"

"No, it's okay. I've been meaning to tell you about it." She paused, steadying her resolve. "I had an operation."

"A serious one, I gather."

"Yes, very serious."

"But you're okay now?" His voice was deep with concern.

"Yes, I'm okay. I had a heart problem."

But suddenly Anna sensed that he was no longer listening to her, that something had drawn his attention away from her. She lifted her head to see what had distracted him.

He was holding the copy of his book that she'd left on the nightstand. Even in the dark, she could see his brooding frown, could feel the way his body had gone suddenly still against her.

"I'm sorry," she murmured. "I should have put it away, but I forgot it was there. Does it bother you to think about…what happened?"

"I think about it all the time." His gaze was still on the book, on the scorpion.

Anna propped herself on her elbow. "Gwen told me that first day that you were still obsessed with the case. She said you'd never gotten over that summer. You're still afraid that Scorpio may come back to finish you off."

He tore his gaze from the book and turned to Anna. There was something in his eyes…in the way he looked at her….

"Gwen was wrong," he said in a strange voice. "Scorpio is dead."

Chapter Fourteen

"Dead?" Anna stared at him in shock. "How do you know that?"

He shrugged. "Call it a hunch. A gut feeling."

"But you don't have proof?"

"No."

Anna glanced at the book. She had a sudden, bizarre notion that the scorpion on the cover was slowly crawling toward her. The skin on the back of her neck prickled at the hallucination. She made herself look away. "Why are you so sure Scorpio is dead then? Because the killings stopped after that summer?"

A muscle throbbed in Ben's jaw. "That's part of it."

"And the other part?"

He turned to her. "Like I said, it's just a hunch."

"In the book, you said you thought Scorpio was female," Anna said softly. "Do you still believe that?"

"Yes."

"And that there were two of them?"

"Yes."

She lay back against the pillows, gooseflesh rippling across her bare skin. She had the sudden need to cover herself, and she reached over the side of the bed for her pajamas. "I keep thinking about all the victims you described in the book. The way they died. The way she tortured and mutilated them. How could someone do that to another human being?"

"There's no good answer to that question, Anna."

"I know. It's just…" She trailed off as she drew on her clothes. "She almost killed you."

His gaze met hers in the darkness. "No. Killing me was never an option for Scorpio. That wasn't part of the game."

"The game?"

"The one we played that summer. The one that would prove who was the more clever and cunning, the more resourceful. I thought I could beat her at her own game, but I was never a match for her. She proved how easily she could get to me, how effortlessly she could take everything from me, and there wasn't a damn thing I could do about it."

While he talked, Ben rose and gathered up his clothing. He dressed swiftly and then lay back down on the bed. "…she destroyed my face, my career, my self-confidence. That was the worst," he said grimly. "She made me lose faith in myself."

"And then you met Katherine," Anna murmured.

He closed his eyes briefly. "I was at my lowest point when we met. I thought it was just a coincidence that she showed up at that book signing."

"Wasn't it?"

He shook his head in disgust. "She arranged it. She arranged everything."

Anna frowned. "How?"

Ben stared at the ceiling. "A few months after I found out I couldn't go back on the force, I got a call from a literary agent. He said he'd been reading about the Scorpio case and thought my story would make a great book. He'd even put out feelers to some publishing houses in New York and had gotten several promising bites. He thought the story had bestseller potential, that it might even be optioned for a movie."

"And what did you say to that?" Anna propped her chin on his chest, gazing up at him.

Absently he stroked her hair. "I told him I wasn't a writer. There was no way I could sit down at the computer and crank out a book. I barely made it through my college English courses." He sighed. "He didn't seem to care. He said that was what ghost-writers were for. He knew someone he thought would be perfect for the job, a protégé of one of his other clients."

"So you agreed."

He shrugged. "I didn't see that I had anything to lose. I had my pension, but not much else. At the very least, collaborating on a book would be a distraction and it seemed easier and cheaper than therapy."

"So you told your story and it became a bestseller, just like the agent predicted," Anna said.

"It was even optioned for a movie. He delivered everything he promised. And then one day, he brought one of his clients—the one who'd recommended the ghostwriter—to one of my book-signings. It was Katherine."

"And your eyes met across the crowded book-store…" Anna murmured.

"Something like that. But it wasn't love. It was never love. To this day, I couldn't tell you what it was. Lust, maybe, but there was something else, too. A connection…" He ran a hand across his eyes as if trying to wipe away a painful memory.

"I'd never met anyone even remotely like her," he said. "She was the most overtly sexual woman I'd ever seen. She couldn't enter a room without every head, male and female, turning in her direction. There was something so completely seductive about the way she walked, the way she carried herself, the way she smiled. I…lost my head over her." He turned away, as if embarrassed by his confession.

"What happened?" Anna prompted.

"We went out to dinner after the autograph session and ended up back in her hotel room." He turned then and cast Anna an uneasy glance. "I won't bore you with the details of that night, or any of the other nights, but fast forward two weeks in time. We got married in Vegas."

He wound a strand of her hair around his finger. "I'm not proud of my behavior, Anna. I'm not proud of anything about that time. It was like…she cast a spell on me or something. I wasn't myself when I was with her. Then the morning after the ceremony, the veil lifted and it was as if I saw her for the first time. The cunning. The subtle hints of cruelty. I'd not only married a woman I didn't know, but one I found I didn't even much like.

"Deep down, I knew I'd made one hell of a mistake, but I kept trying to convince myself regrets and second thoughts were normal in situations like that. It might still work out. So I agreed to move into her house here in San Miguel, partly because I was hoping I was wrong about her, and partly because I had nothing to go back to in Houston.

"But when I saw her with her daughter…the way she treated Gabby…" His features tightened in anger. "I knew there wasn't any hope for us. I couldn't live with a woman who could do that to any child, let alone to her own."

Anna's stomach recoiled at his story. "What did she do to Gabby?" she whispered.

"It was nothing obvious. Nothing physical. At least not that I ever knew about. But it was abuse, nonetheless. A constant erosion of Gabby's self-confidence. Katherine was trying to take from her exactly what Scorpio had taken from me, and there was no way I could let her do that to Gabby. But I didn't have any legal claim, and if I'd left, I knew Katherine would never let me see her again. So I was trapped in that house, just as Gabby was, and, of course, that was what Katherine had wanted all along."

"And then she died."

Ben's gaze burned into hers. "I didn't kill her, Anna. I swear it."

"I never thought you did. But someone killed her. And you know who it was, don't you?"

"The police ruled her death a suicide," he said, but he couldn't quite meet her gaze.

"But it wasn't, was it?" And who better to make

it look like a suicide than a cop? Wasn't that what both Emily and Mendoza had warned her about?

"Don't jump to conclusions, Anna," he said darkly.

"I'm not." She hesitated, putting her hand on his arm. "Gabby killed her mother, didn't she?"

Ben closed his eyes briefly. "I don't know for sure. I wasn't there when it happened. I came later…" He paused, wiping his hand across his mouth. "Gabby had been acting strangely for days. Strange even for her. I knew something was on her mind, but she wouldn't talk to me about it. Then late one afternoon, I saw her head toward the river. I don't know why, but something made me check the gun cabinet in the study. Katherine's .38 was missing. I don't know if I thought Gabby was going to hurt herself or what. I don't know if I was thinking at all, I just…reacted. By the time I got to the river, she was heading upstream. I knew where she was going. She and Katherine both spent a lot of time at the mission. There was no other boat, so I had to go back for my car, drive into town, and cross the bridge. When I got to the mission, Gabby came running out. She was covered in blood and so hysterical, I could hardly make sense of what she was saying. When I finally got her calmed down, I sent her back across the river to call for help. Then I went inside the mission."

"You somehow made Katherine's death look like a suicide," Anna whispered.

"I didn't have to. She'd been shot in the head at pointblank range with her own .38. She had powder burns and residue on her skin that were consistent with a self-inflicted gunshot wound. And the gun was still in her hand.''

''Are you telling me that Gabby knew how to arrange the crime scene to make it look like a suicide?'' Anna asked incredulously. ''She was only thirteen years old!''

''She's her mother's daughter,'' Ben said, and a chill ran up Anna's spine. ''But it's possible Katherine really did take her own life.''

''You don't believe it, do you? And neither does Mendoza. He suspects you did something to the crime scene, but he's never been able to prove it. And that's why he doesn't like you.''

''That's only one of many reasons why Mendoza doesn't like me,'' Ben said dryly. ''He was in love with Katherine for years.''

My God, Anna thought. What kind of unnatural allure had that woman possessed that had caused everyone who crossed her path to fall in love with her?

''The ambulance took Katherine to a level one trauma unit in San Antonio,'' Ben was saying. ''By the time I got there, Gwen was already in the emergency waiting room. One of the doctors came out to inform us that Katherine was clinically brain dead and was being kept alive on life support. A few hours later, someone else came out to talk to us about organ donation. They had Katherine's name in the database, but they still wanted permission from the next of kin.''

''And you gave it to them.''

''Yes, although Gwen was dead-set against it.''

"Why?"

He shrugged, but something dark came into his eyes. "She had her reasons."

Anna drew a deep breath. Now it was her turn. "Did you ever hear from any of the transplant recipients?"

He shook his head. "No. But the hospital told me that someone was waiting for one of her kidneys."

"What about her heart?"

"I don't know if anyone got her heart."

"Someone did," Anna said quietly. "Someone did get her heart."

"What?" He turned to stare at her for a moment and then his gaze dropped to her chest as if he was picturing the scar beneath her pajamas. Anna saw something dawn in his eyes that looked very much like horror. "You? You have her heart?"

When she nodded, he rose from the bed and backed away from her. Anna had tried to prepare herself for his reaction, his shock, but she hadn't been ready for this. He couldn't stand to be near her. Even in the dark, she could see his revulsion. It made her want to curl up and die.

But she was nothing if not a survivor. She rose to her knees. "I'm sorry I didn't tell you before—"

"Why *didn't* you tell me?" he cut in coldly. He ran a hand through his hair, staring down at her in disbelief. "Why did you come here? What do you want?"

"Nothing. I don't want anything. Just…your understanding."

"Understanding?" He glared at her. "I can't believe you did this. Why the deception? Why not just tell the truth?''

"Because both the donor's and the transplant recipient's identities are kept anonymous for a reason. It's to protect all parties involved. When you didn't respond to my letter, I assumed you didn't want to meet me—''

"Wait a minute. What letter?"

"All transplant recipients are encouraged to write a letter to the donor's family. It's delivered anonymously through the hospital. When you didn't respond, I assumed you wanted no further communication.''

"I never received your letter," he said. "But if you assumed I didn't want to meet with you, why come here? Why force it?"

"I wasn't going to force it," Anna tried to explain. "I didn't tell you who I was because I wanted to respect your privacy. I didn't want the meeting to be awkward for you, or to…dredge up painful memories. All I wanted to do was meet Katherine's family. To find out about her life.''

"Why?"

The word was an indictment, and he'd already found her guilty. Anna wasn't sure what she could say to make things right. "I know it's hard for anyone who hasn't been in my position to understand, but it was something I had to do. I had to find out whether or not I deserved Katherine's heart.''

Ben said nothing to that. Anna thought he must still be in a state of shock.

He lifted his hands to his face. "My God. You have her heart. You of all people..."

"I know." Anna closed her eyes briefly. "But I'm not her, Ben. A heart is just muscle and tissue. It has nothing to do with who I am. I don't have her soul."

He lowered his hands from his face, as if something had just occurred to him. "But what if you do?"

It was Anna's turn to stare in shock. "What?"

"What if there is something of her inside you? Some...essence of who she was. *What* she was."

"That's insane. I'm still the same woman I was before the surgery."

"Are you?"

Anna put a hand to her mouth, trying to quell the terrible emotions churning inside her. She *wasn't* the same woman she'd been before the surgery. She'd changed, so much so she hardly recognized herself at times. But it had nothing to do with Katherine's heart. It couldn't.

"How do you explain this thing between us?" Ben demanded. "From the moment I first met you it was as if I already knew you. We had a connection. You can't deny that."

"But it's not because of her heart," Anna said desperately. "It can't be."

"But how do you know? How can *I* know?" He moved to the bed and took her by the shoulders, staring deep into her eyes. "How do I know you won't eventually become her?"

"That's crazy—"

"Is it? She was the most cunningly vicious woman I ever met. How do I know that she didn't somehow orchestrate this whole thing? That making me fall in love with you was part of the game, her final move?''

Anna went very still on the outside, but her heart—Katherine's heart—suddenly pounded in terror against her chest. ''What are you saying, Ben?''

''Don't you understand? Don't you get it?''

And then, as she stared up into his eyes, the revelation hit her. She gasped in shock, in denial, in gut-wrenching horror. ''No,'' she whispered. ''No…'' But she could see the truth in Ben's eyes.

Katherine Sprague and Scorpio were one and the same woman.

Chapter Fifteen

Anna watched Ben slip silently through the French doors and disappear into the shadows on the balcony. She didn't try to get him to stay. She knew why he couldn't. Knew why he couldn't look at her, touch her, couldn't stand to be in the same room with her.

She had Katherine's heart.

Scorpio's heart.

Anna put a hand to her chest and felt the steady rhythm of her heart. *Her* heart, she tried to tell herself.

But what if Ben was right? What if some essence of Katherine had been transplanted along with her heart? What if Anna now possessed some of the dead woman's cruelty, her cunning? Her psychopathic urge to kill?

How about it, Anna? Had any strange cravings since your surgery?

Hays's taunt suddenly came back to Anna and she realized she'd completely forgotten about Laurel's concern that he might be trying to find her. Her ex-husband's obsession—if that's what it was—suddenly seemed the least of Anna's worries.

She had Katherine's heart. Scorpio's heart.

The heart of a serial killer beat inside her chest, and Ben would never be able to look at her in the same way again.

He hated her, you know. My mother. He despised her. He wanted her dead…he'll want you dead, too, when he finds out.

It was Gabby's words tormenting her now, and Anna paced the small confines of the room, bombarded by self-doubts. Consumed with fear. But she wasn't afraid for herself any longer. She was afraid, suddenly, for everyone around her.

"How do I know you won't eventually become her?"

BEN MELTED into the shadows on the balcony, leaning his head against the wall as he squeezed his eyes closed. Anna had Katherine's heart. Scorpio's heart.

He put a fist to his head as he tried to think what to do about that.

He'd handled the situation badly. He knew that. He'd made all sorts of baseless accusations and bizarre leaps of logic. Katherine was dead. She couldn't come back. Not in any form. A heart couldn't hold memory, couldn't retain the essence of its human host. Once removed from the body, it became merely an organ. Muscle and tissue, as Anna had said.

But…what about the attraction between him and Anna? The instant connection? From the moment Ben had set eyes on Anna it was as if he knew her, as if he'd been waiting his whole life for her. Could all that be just a coincidence, some strange twist of fate?

Or was it more diabolical than that? Had Katherine

somehow arranged before her death for Anna to receive her heart? Had she planned the whole thing, knowing that Anna would come to San Miguel to meet her family, anticipating that she and Ben would fall in love...and that his finding out about her heart would be the cruelest joke of all?

That was insane, and he knew it. Katherine had been evil, but she couldn't predict what the future would hold. She hadn't possessed any supernatural powers. Just cunning and cruelty and a bloodlust that had made her the most vicious killer Ben had ever come across as a cop.

And now Anna had her heart.

Anna had her heart, and whether Ben wanted to admit it or not, there were similarities between the two women. Both possessed an extraordinary beauty. Both were clever and deceptive. And he'd been fooled by both of them.

He spotted one of Mendoza's men making his rounds and Ben pressed himself against the wall, not wanting to get caught outside of Anna's room. The last thing he needed tonight was to be hauled off to jail.

He glanced toward Anna's room. He wanted to go back inside and somehow make things right between them, but knowing what he now knew, Ben wasn't at all sure things could ever be right again. He wasn't sure he could ever look at her in the same way, but the one thing he did know was that he would do whatever was necessary to keep her safe.

She might have Katherine's heart, but she was still Anna. And he was still in love with her.

Someone had tried to kill her earlier, and Ben was starting to have a bad feeling that maybe he wasn't the only one who knew whose heart beat inside her chest.

ANNA BARELY SLEPT at all that night, and the next morning, she rose from bed groggy and exhausted. She showered and dressed, then glanced around the tiny room. She didn't have the foggiest idea of what to do with herself for the rest of the day. Her car wouldn't be ready until Tuesday. Maybe she should take Mendoza's advice and go back to Houston as soon as possible. She still wasn't certain she would be any safer there, but at least she wouldn't run the risk of running into Ben.

The memory of his disgust tore at Anna's fragile resolve. She didn't want to fall apart. Not now. Not when she needed to remain strong and in control. She needed the old Anna more than ever now.

A knock sounded on her door, and she opened it to find Margarete outside with fresh towels and sheets draped across her arm.

"Should I come back later to clean your room?" she wanted to know. Her dark gaze flicked over Anna's shoulder as if she were expecting to find someone else in Anna's room.

"No, it's okay," Anna said quickly. "I'll just wait out on the balcony. The fresh air will do me good."

"As you wish."

Anna stepped out on the balcony and then glanced over her shoulder. Margarete was still in the doorway watching her, evidently waiting for her to vacate the room completely before she began tidying up.

The woman was an enigma, Anna decided, as she found a chair in the shade and sat down. But then so many people in San Miguel seemed to have some sort of mystery about them. And one of them had tried to kill her.

She shivered as her gaze scanned the grounds. She saw Acacia talking to one of the police officers, but Ben was nowhere in sight. She hadn't expected to see him today. It wouldn't surprise her if she never saw him again, but the thought made her unbearably sad. It was true they'd known each other for only a few short days, but it didn't seem that way. Anna felt as if she'd been waiting her whole life for a man like Ben.

A breeze drifted along the balcony, carrying a breath of coolness and a hint of rain. Anna could hear Acacia's throaty laughter from the grounds below and the more distant drone of a lawn mower. The sounds were peaceful, innocent. She tilted her head back and closed her eyes. She was so exhausted, she could almost be lulled to sleep.

There was another sound, too. The faint tinkle of a piano. Acacia must be giving a lesson, Anna thought drowsily.

And then she heard Acacia's laughter again.

Anna's eyes flew open. She rose from her chair and looked over the railing. Acacia was still on the grounds flirting with the police officer. She couldn't be giving a lesson....

The sound wasn't coming from the music room

below, Anna suddenly realized, but from farther down the balcony. A door in the other wing had been left ajar, and she could see the sheer curtain stirring gently in the breeze.

She turned again toward the grounds. Acacia and the officer were still down there, well within shouting distance, as was Margarete.

Anna edged along the balcony toward the open doorway. She only wanted to glance into the room, but she wasn't sure she had the nerve to advance much farther. Not alone. For all she knew the person who had tried to kill her was inside that room, luring her with the music, waiting to cut out her heart.

A grisly thought for such a sunny morning, Anna decided. She glanced around to make sure the cop was still visible, still within earshot. He glanced up and saw her then and started walking across the grounds toward her.

"Is everything okay?" he called up.

"Yes, I think so." She paused. "Could you just wait right there for a moment?"

He frowned up at her. "Are you sure you're okay, Ms. Sebastian?"

"Yes, I'm fine. Just…please wait there for a moment." She turned and hurried along the balcony. The music was definitely coming from the hotel room. She paused just outside the doorway, straining to see inside.

A stray gust of wind stirred the curtains and lifted a piece of paper lying on the balcony. Anna caught the torn photograph before it blew away. And when she turned it over, she drew in a sharp breath, the blood in her veins going icy cold. It was her wedding photo. Hays had been cut out, and a crude heart with a jagged line running up the middle had been drawn on Anna's chest.

She glanced back down at the cop. Acacia had joined him, and they were chatting again. When she saw Anna staring at them, a tiny, knowing smiled curled her lips.

Anna hurried back along the balcony to her own room. ''Margarete?''

The older woman was making the bed. She turned when she heard her name. ''Yes?''

''The man in the other wing. Mr. Carter, you called him. What does he look like?''

''I don't understand—''

''Just tell me what he looks like,'' Anna said impatiently. ''Tall, short, thin, heavy. What?''

Margarete paused. ''He's not tall,'' she finally said. ''Under six feet. Thin, but muscular. Dark hair cut very short. Blue eyes.''

Hays. He was here.

''Could you come with me for a minute? Please,'' Anna said when the woman hesitated. ''It'll only take a moment.''

Reluctantly, Margarete followed her along the balcony to the open doorway. The music was still playing.

''There isn't a piano in that room, is there?'' Anna asked.

''It must be the radio,'' Margarete said. She moved past Anna and glanced into the room. ''Mr. Carter? Is everything okay?''

No answer.

Margarete took a step into the room. "Mr. Carter?"

"You didn't see him leave this morning?" Anna asked uneasily.

"No."

Margarete's curiosity seemed to overcome her then, and she walked into the room, glancing around. "I'll check the bathroom to see if he needs fresh towels," she murmured.

While Margarete went into the bathroom, Anna glanced around the bedroom. The space was almost unnaturally tidy, and she remembered that Hays had always been something of a neat freak. But this room was so orderly, it was like no one had ever been inside.

Margarete came out of the bathroom and started toward the door. "Everything is fine. He must have just stepped out for a few moments. He may be downstairs."

"Where is the music coming from?" Anna murmured. "Do you see a radio?"

"No." Margarete looked suddenly uneasy. "Please. We should leave now. We can't intrude on his privacy any longer."

But Anna was already at the bathroom door, peaking inside. As Margarete said, nothing seemed amiss. The towels were all neatly folded on a shelf above the toilet, the sink spotless to the point of antiseptic.

The only flaw in the room was a dripping faucet behind the shower curtain. Without thinking, Anna reached over and pulled the panel back.

And there was Hays.

Covered in blood.

He had a gaping hole in his chest where his heart had been removed. He stared up at Anna with unseeing eyes, and then in horror, she realized something had been stuffed into his mouth. A scorpion...

She screamed then and staggered back, straight into Margarete.

"Dios mío!" the woman muttered, crossing herself as her gaze fixed on the dead man.

Anna ran out of the room and somehow managed to call for the officer before she collapsed onto the balcony, so sick with shock and horror, she couldn't lift her head for a very long time.

ANNA'S HANDS shook so badly she could hardly hold the glass of water someone had brought to her. She sat on the bench in the lobby, trying to keep her thoughts organized enough to answer Mendoza's questions.

He'd been summoned by Margarete, and over Mendoza's protests, Anna had summoned Ben. Hays's death—or more specifically, the way he'd died—was something Ben needed to know about.

Anna tried to block the images that were still raging inside her head, but she kept seeing Hays's eyes. That awful hole in his chest. The scorpion...

Her stomach revolted once again, and she worried for a moment that she would need to excuse herself.

With an effort, she beat back the nausea and tried to focus on Detective Mendoza. She didn't dare look at Ben. She didn't want to see what might be in his eyes this morning. Disgust. Horror. Maybe even suspicion.

"So let me see if I'm clear on this," Mendoza was saying. His gaze was dark and probing. "The victim, who was registered here as John Carter, was in reality a man named Hays Devereaux."

"Yes, that's right." Anna clasped her hands in a vain attempt to keep them from trembling.

"And you know this because you were once married to the deceased. Is that correct?"

Anna still didn't glance at Ben, but she could feel his gaze on her. She knew what he must have been thinking. What else had she kept from him?

"What do you think he was doing in San Miguel?" Mendoza asked.

"He must have followed me. I can't think why else he would be here."

"Are you sure it wasn't the other way around?" Mendoza pressed. "I've done some checking. His company has oil leases in the area. Could it be that you followed him to San Miguel?"

Anna stared at him in astonishment. She did look at Ben then, but he glanced away the moment her gaze touched his. She turned back to Mendoza. "I didn't follow my ex-husband here, Detective. We've been divorced for years."

"And you've had no contact since then?"

"No, not since—" The day Dr. English was murdered.

"Yes?"

"I saw him recently, but only briefly."

"Was it a friendly meeting?"

"Not particularly," Anna said.

"You wouldn't say, then, that your divorce was an amicable one?"

"It was not."

He scribbled something in his notebook, then glanced back up. "There's something I've never been quite clear on, Ms. Sebastian. Perhaps you can help me out. If you didn't follow your ex-husband to San Miguel, why did you come here?"

Anna drew a breath. "I came here to pay my respects to Katherine Sprague's family."

"Yes. That's what I hear. But somehow that doesn't quite ring true for me."

"It is the truth." Anna glanced at Ben again, and this time, he didn't look away. There was something in his eyes, an emotion Anna wanted to believe was sympathy, but somehow she didn't think it was.

"You've had some health problems recently, haven't you?" Mendoza asked.

Anna moistened her lips. "Yes."

"May I inquire as to the nature of your illness?"

"I had a heart transplant."

"Who was your doctor?"

Anna almost gasped out loud. She was an attorney, for God's sake. She should have seen that trap before it was sprung. "Dr. Michael English."

Her gaze flickered to Ben. He was clearly stunned by the revelation.

"Correct me if I'm wrong, but Dr. English is also dead."

"Yes."

"Murdered?"

"Yes."

"So your doctor is dead. Your ex-husband is dead. A young woman you befriended has gone missing. People around you seem to be dropping like flies, Ms. Sebastian."

"What is it you're implying, Detective Mendoza?" Anna steeled her voice and tried to sharpen her claws, but unfortunately, she'd been away from the courtroom too long. She was out of practice, and her illness had dulled her edge. Shock had also taken a toll. She was doing the one thing she would have advised her clients to never do. She was talking to the police without benefit of counsel.

"I'm not implying anything," Mendoza told her. "I'm merely trying to get to the bottom of a very ugly murder."

"Are you forgetting that an attempt was made on my life last evening?" she asked coolly.

"And as I recall, I advised you to return to Houston. Now I find myself in the awkward position of having to rescind that advice. I must ask that you not leave town until further notice." He stood, drawing the interview to a conclusion.

Ben waited until Mendoza was out of earshot before turning to Anna. "Are you okay?"

"I don't know," she said numbly. She glanced up at him. "What's happening around here, Ben? Why was Hays murdered? Why was he even here?"

"He was murdered for the same reason Michael English was killed," Ben said grimly. "And for all we know, for the same reason Emily Winsome has gone missing. They're all tied to you."

Anna's blood turned to ice. "You think I did it, don't you?" she whispered. "You think I've become her. Katherine."

He drew a hand through his hair. "Look, I said some crazy things last night. I wasn't thinking clearly. When you told me about the transplant…I freaked. It was the last thing I expected, and I didn't handle it very well."

Anna held her breath, waiting.

"You should have told me the truth from the beginning," he said.

"I realize that now. But when I first came here, I never dreamed that you and I—" She stopped suddenly. But she *had* dreamed about Ben. She'd dreamed about being with him just as they had been last night.

"You never dreamed what?"

She shook her head. "It doesn't matter. I'm just sorry I messed things up so badly."

"There's nothing we can do about it now," he said wearily. "What we have to concentrate on now is keeping you safe. I've talked to Mendoza. He's posting a guard inside the hotel and another two on the grounds. You should be safe enough here tonight. I don't think the killer would dare come back."

"Not even Scorpio?"

His gaze darkened. "Scorpio is dead."

"But you said there were two of them. Scorpio's partner is still alive, isn't she?" And then it hit Anna like the proverbial ton of bricks. She knew, suddenly, why Ben had stayed on in San Miguel. It wasn't just for Gabby's sake, although it was obvious he cared about her. He'd known all along the other one was here. He'd stayed to use himself as bait to try and lure the second killer out of hiding. "You know who it is, don't you?" she whispered.

He couldn't quite meet her gaze suddenly. "Stay in your room tonight, Anna. Don't let anyone in."

"Where will you be?" she asked worriedly.

"I've contacted someone I know at the FBI. He worked with me on the Scorpio cases, and he's agreed to come down here and take a look at what we've got. He's catching the first available flight out of Dulles. I'm driving to San Antonio later to pick him up."

"Ben." She caught his arm, and to her intense relief, he didn't shake her off. "Be careful. Maybe the killer is laying a very clever trap for you. Maybe she's killing people connected to me to throw the police off her trail. Maybe the person Scorpio really wants is still you."

He stared down at her for a moment, his gaze deep and fathomless. And then he said very softly, "Scorpio is dead, Anna."

But something that might have been dread flickered in his eyes before he turned away.

Chapter Sixteen

Anna went straight up to her room after dinner. She hadn't been able to eat a bite, but the cup of tea she'd ordered had helped to settle her stomach a little.

Once inside her room, she made sure the doors were locked, then crossed the room to stare out at the grounds. Dusk had fallen, but she could still see the silhouette of one of the guards Mendoza had posted outside the hotel. He was standing at the top of the steps that led down to the dock. Another was inside the hotel.

Anna knew that Mendoza must have severely stretched the San Miguel police force for this assignment, but she didn't delude herself into thinking that her safety was that important to him. Last night, he'd put his men here to insure that no one could get into the Casa del Gatos. Tonight she had a feeling he wanted to make sure she didn't get out.

Did he really believe she'd killed Hays?

Did Ben?

After her interview earlier with Mendoza, Ben seemed to regret some of the things he'd said the night before. But he *had* said them. In the heat of the moment, so to speak. And wasn't that when a person was most likely to say what was really on his mind or in his heart?

She had Katherine's heart, and Katherine had been a killer. Not just a killer, but a cunning manipulator. She'd lured Ben into her deadly game, and then when she'd taken away everything that had meant anything to him, she'd set out to seduce him.

What must it have been like for him when he'd come to the horrifying realization that the woman he'd married was the same brutal killer he'd been tracking for years?

And now Anna had her heart.

Turning away from the window, she went through the motions of getting ready for bed. It was still early, and she knew it would be hours yet before she would fall asleep, if she slept at all.

But the routine of washing her face, brushing her teeth and taking her evening meds was comforting somehow. It gave her something to focus on, for a few minutes at least, besides the killer.

Changing into her pajamas, she climbed into bed and pulled the covers up over her.

Anna had no idea how long she lay there before she began to get drowsy. The feeling surprised her. She was exhausted, and she hadn't slept well for two nights running, but she didn't think tonight, of all nights, she'd be able to sleep a wink. But all of a sudden, her eyes were so heavy she couldn't keep them open. Maybe she'd just close them for a moment…

When she woke up, someone was sitting on the edge of her bed, calling her name softly.

"Wake up, Anna. Come on. It's time to go."

Anna was so groggy and disoriented, she couldn't think why someone would be visiting her so late. She couldn't quite tell—

"Come on, Anna. Wake up!"

The feminine voice was firmer now, and suddenly very familiar. Familiar...but strange...

The figure on her bed was just a blur. Anna blinked, but she couldn't bring her into focus.

She slapped Anna's cheeks. "Anna! Wake up! It's time to go!"

"Wh—" Anna's tongue was so thick she couldn't form words around it.

"You'll see. Now come on." She tugged on Anna's arms. "Up you go. Hurry now. We don't have a lot of time."

Even in her drugged state, Anna held back.

The voice grew angry. "I'm losing my patience with you, Anna. Come on. Ben's waiting for us."

That one word, Ben's name, seemed to penetrate Anna's foggy brain. She clutched at it like a drowning man hanging on to a life raft. "Ben?"

"I knew that would get your attention," the voice murmured. "Come on. Up you go." She pulled Anna to her feet and wrapped Anna's arm around her neck, staggering a bit under her weight. "That's it. Just put one foot in front of the other. Good girl. Ben will be so proud."

Ben. She was going to see Ben.

But...would Ben want to see her?

Anna balked again at the French door.

"You're going to have to give me a little cooperation here." The voice sounded strained from holding up Anna's weight. "Come on, Anna. I thought you wanted to see Ben. He's waiting for us. If we don't hurry, he could be in danger. You don't want anything to happen to Ben, do you? No, I didn't think so. Okay, that's the way. Just a few more steps and we're out the door."

Ben was in danger? No...

They were on the balcony now. Anna could feel a hot breeze on her face, but it did little to chase away the haze. She still couldn't think...couldn't seem to concentrate.

Ben was in danger.

"Police," she whispered.

"Don't worry about the police," the voice said. "A little something in the coffee pot took care of them. But they won't be out forever. We still have to hurry...."

Anna stood at the top of the steps, looking down. The ground seemed a long way off. Much, much too far. She'd never make it...she was too dizzy....

"Come on," the voice urged.

Anna put one foot in front of the other, and then without warning, pitched forward. Mercifully, she was unconscious by the time she hit the bottom.

SHE CAME TO PERIODICALLY, but the pain was so intense, she welcomed the darkness. Once, she had the sensation of being dragged on the ground. Another time, she thought she was in a boat. When she was finally able to fight the pain and remain conscious for more than a few seconds, she opened her eyes to the flickering glow of candlelight.

For a split second, Anna thought she was dreaming and Ben would appear any moment.

But she hurt too badly to be dreaming. No, this was reality. A strange reality, but it was happening to her nonetheless.

Surprisingly the pain from the fall seemed to have cleared her head somewhat. When she glanced around, she realized at once that she was lying on the dirt floor in the mission. Candles and flowers had been placed at various points around the room. It was as if someone had prepared the place for a romantic interlude.

Or a funeral.

Her funeral.

The pain had helped clear her head, but she still couldn't move, Anna realized. She was lying on her side, her wrists and ankles bound behind her. She struggled for a moment until she realized it was useless.

Someone was coming toward her. As she knelt beside Anna, candlelight sparked off the knife she held in her hand.

Emily said softly, "It's a shame you had to come to. It would have been much easier for you if you'd stayed under. But I'll try to make it quick for your sake. Quicker than the others because I like you."

"Why—" Anna could barely speak. She wasn't sure if it was the residue of drugs in her system or sheer terror.

"Because Katherine's heart has to be left here, where it should have been all along."

Emily rose and began to pace around the room, pausing at each candle to stare down at the floor. When she came back to Anna, her eyes were gleaming with madness.

"The others are here, waiting. All those hearts. The ones I gave to Katherine to prove how much I loved her." She waved an arm around the room. "This is a valentine to her. A secret valentine."

And suddenly, Anna understood. There were thirteen candles in the room, one for each of Scorpio's victims, and one for Emily's victim. Hays's heart was here, too. All the hearts were here.

Oh, God. Oh, dear God...

The uneven floor made sense now. The tiny mounds were graves of a sort.

Horror rising like bile in her throat, Anna struggled against the cords, tried to scream through her terror but the sound came out hardly more than a muffled whimper.

Emily put the knife blade against her mouth. "Shush. Be quiet." She lifted her head as if listening to the silence. "Do you hear them?"

Anna listened, hoping and praying to hear sounds of a rescue. She heard nothing.

"You don't hear them?" Emily asked incredulously. "Listen close. They're still beating. All of them."

A chill ran up Anna's spine. Her eyes widened in terror.

"And now Katherine's heart will finally join them, in our special place. The way it was meant to be."

Anna strained at the cords, pulled with all her might, but it was no use. She was going to die here...in the same place where Katherine had been shot so that Anna could live.

The irony was devastating.

"Don't try to fight it," Emily whispered. "No one can hear you out here. No one will be looking for you, either. They think you're safe and sound up in your room. The guards are probably still out. I put the drug in the pot of coffee Margarete made for them. Just like I put it in your medication. You're a good girl, Anna. I knew you'd take your evening meds."

"Ben—"

Emily smiled. "You're hoping he'll come and save you, aren't you? But he can't. He can't save anyone, Anna. He couldn't even save himself. And I should know," she said with a secretive smile. She lifted the knife to her face, mimicking the line of Ben's scar.

Something seemed to change in her demeanor. The soft, dreamy persona disappeared, and in its place, Anna sensed a savage cunning. For the first time, she glimpsed the killer in Emily.

"Everything was so perfect until he came along. Katherine loved me. She told me how special I was, how pretty I was. She'd never met anyone like me. She made me do things for her to prove my love for her, but I didn't mind because she taught me things. Wonderful things. She made me fall in love with her and then—"

"You killed her," a voice said from the doorway.

Anna saw his silhouette in the doorway, and a rush of emotions swept over her.

Emily had turned toward the sound, too. And now, suddenly, she had something Anna hadn't noticed before. A gun...

She tried to scream a warning, tried to tear at her bonds. She'd never felt so helpless in her life.

"Why did you do it?" Ben said softly. "Why did you kill those people for her?"

"I had to."

"Why?"

"Because...she told me to."

"You know what?" Ben's voice was soft, steady, unafraid. "I understand that. Katherine had a way about her. She could make you do things you didn't want to. She used us both, Emily."

"She said she loved me, but she didn't. Not after you came along. She said I was ugly and stupid and no one would ever want me. 'Do you think I could ever love anyone like you? How dumb are you? My skin crawls just looking at you...'"

"How did it happen?" Ben urged.

"I asked her to meet me here. I had her gun. I'd slipped inside the house and taken it. When she saw it, she just laughed. Laughed in my face. Told me I'd never be able to use it, she said. Not unless she told me to. I wouldn't be able to do anything without her. I might as well put the gun barrel in my mouth and pull the trigger." Emily's voice faltered, then grew stronger. "She took the gun and put it to her head. Then she put my hand over hers. 'Do it,' she said. 'Pull the trigger.' But I couldn't and she knew it. She started laughing. She kept on laughing...."

"So you did it," Ben said. "You pulled the trigger."

"I had to. She told me to."

"Katherine's not here now, Emily. So why don't you put the gun down?"

"I can't. I have to finish my valentine to her. Then

we'll always be together. I can come here and talk to her anytime I want. I'll bring her presents just like I used to...."

Slowly she turned to Anna and lifted the gun.

Before she could pull the trigger, Ben fired from the doorway. The first shot went wild, because of his injury, but the second hit its mark dead-on.

BEN CAME TO SEE ANNA every day that she was in the hospital. Luckily, she hadn't broken any bones in the fall, and the drug Emily had put in her medication hadn't caused any lingering effects. But the best news of all was that her heart biopsies had detected no signs of rejection.

Health-wise, she was going to be fine, but mentally she was a wreck. It wasn't just the terror and horror she'd experienced that night in the mission that tormented her. It was knowing that the heart that beat inside her chest had once belonged to a cold-blooded killer. It was knowing that every time Ben looked at her, he saw Katherine.

He didn't say that, of course. But Anna knew. She could see it in his eyes, in the way he kept his distance. In the way he refused to touch her....

After the first couple of days, when he knew she was going to be okay, he began to tell her everything he'd learned about the case. Since both Emily and Katherine were dead, much of their motivation was still guesswork, but Gwen had been able to supply Ben and the FBI profiler with some valuable insight into Katherine's background.

Katherine had been extraordinarily beautiful even as a child, and her father had wanted her all to himself. Katherine's mother not only turned a blind eye to the abuse, but would sometimes watch. And then afterwards, consumed by jealousy, she'd blamed Katherine and would often beat her until she was nearly unconscious.

When their parents died in a fire, Gwen always secretly suspected that Katherine had killed them. She loved her sister, but over the years, she began to see traits in Katherine that frightened her. The cunning. The cruelty. The pleasure she derived from inflicting pain, both physical and mental, on others.

"She couldn't distinguish pleasure from pain," Ben said. "After what her parents did to her, she couldn't experience one without the other."

"And all those women she had Emily kill for her... Katherine was having her mother killed over and over again, wasn't she? She was cutting out her mother's heart."

"It's possible," he said grimly. "But we'll never know for sure."

"What was the significance of the scorpions?"

"I think that goes back to something Gwen told me. She said that when she was a child Katherine used to tell her the fable of the scorpion and the frog. Do you remember it?"

"Vaguely."

"A scorpion and frog were on the bank of a river. The scorpion asked the frog to give him a ride on his back across the water, but the frog was afraid the scorpion would sting him. The scorpion assured the frog he wouldn't because they'd both die if he did. Halfway across the river, the scorpion stung the frog. When the frog asked why, the scorpion said, 'Because I'm a scorpion. It's my nature.'"

"So Katherine knew even back then what she was."

"And Emily?"

"Her background is pretty sketchy, but the best we can tell, the state took her away from an abusive home when she was four or five. The welfare workers found her chained inside a closet where she was sometimes kept for days on end as punishment. She lived in a series of foster homes after that, but was never adopted. When she and Katherine met, they each saw something in the other that they'd been searching for for a long time. Katherine, someone willing to kill for her, and Emily, someone to love her."

"Why did Emily kill Michael?" Anna asked.

"It was probably symbolic," Ben said. "He's the one who gave you Katherine's heart."

"And Hays?"

"She was afraid he'd take you away before she could complete her mission. Her valentine, she called it."

"That's why she came back here. To finish her valentine to Katherine." That was why she'd lured Anna to San Miguel by playing "Heart and Soul" over the phone to her. She could have learned Anna's identity as easily as Gabby had.

"She pretended to be searching for Katherine's killer so that she would have a reason to stay in San Miguel," Ben said. "And to throw the police off track."

Anna shuddered. "I never knew love could be so twisted. Or so complicated." She hesitated, her gaze seeking his. "Out of all this horror, do you think it's possible…that something good can come from it?"

Ben walked over to her bed and stood staring down at her. "I don't know, Anna. I honestly don't know."

LAUREL LOOKED UP from her packing as Anna came into the room and sat on the edge of the bed. "Are you sure about this, Anna?"

"Yes. I'm very sure. You need to get back to your own home and your own life, Laurel. I can take care of myself now. The doctors gave me a clean bill of health. I'm fine."

"Fine? You were almost killed…when I think about what almost happened…" Laurel's eyes filled with tears.

Anna reached up and took her stepmother's hand. "I really am going to be okay, Laurel. But I never could have made it this far without you. What you've done for me…I'll never be able to repay you. And after the way I treated you for all those years… You could have just turned your back on me."

"Oh, Anna, I could never do that. Not when I see your father every time I look in those big brown eyes…." She smiled wistfully. "He would have been so proud of you."

Anna winced. "I'm not so sure about that. I never gave him much reason to be proud."

"But you did. And he was. More than you'll ever know. You're a wonderful person, Anna. You've just never given yourself a chance. You've been so afraid of getting hurt."

"Well, maybe it's time I gave myself that chance," Anna murmured. "After all, I may not get many more."

"Don't talk like that," Laurel admonished. She

went back to her packing, but when the doorbell rang, she automatically turned to answer it.

"No, I'll get it." Anna rose from the bed. "You've waited on me long enough."

The doorbell sounded again as she hurried down the hallway. "Hold on," she muttered. "I'm coming."

She drew back the door and there stood Ben.

She hadn't seen him in over a week. Not since she'd come home from the hospital.

She'd begun to think...

They didn't say anything for a long moment, just stood staring at each other until finally Anna stepped back to allow him to enter.

"I wasn't sure I'd ever see you again," she finally managed.

He glanced around her apartment, as if suddenly at a loss. "Nice place."

"Thanks. Would you...like to come in and sit down?" She showed him to the living room, but when she sat down on the sofa, Ben remained standing.

He walked over to the window to stare out. "Nice view."

"You didn't come here to compliment my apartment," she said. "Did you?"

He turned. He looked tired, Anna noticed, as if he hadn't slept in days. She knew the feeling.

"I've moved back to Houston," he said abruptly.

Anna's brows lifted. "What about Gabby?"

"I've asked her to come live with me, but she wants to stay with Gwen. She says Gwen will be lost without her. I have a feeling she's right about that."

"Do you think she'll be okay?"

"She and Gwen are both in counseling. They're selling the house and moving here so that I can keep an eye on Gabby. I want to be a part of her life. I want to do everything I can to help her, to keep her from becoming—" He broke off, turning away.

"You will be able to help her, Ben. Gabby's not her mother."

He glanced at her. "I know that."

"And I'm not Katherine. I don't have her soul. I don't have any part of her except her heart. And it's my heart now."

"I know that, too."

"So where does that leave us, Ben?" she asked softly.

He came to sit beside her, taking her hands in his. "That's why I'm here. I thought I should tell you my plans and then we can…figure out the rest together."

The rest?

"I've taken a job with BMI—"

"BMI?" she cut in.

"It's a private investigation firm—"

"I know what it is," Anna said. "It's the firm I used to find out the identity of my donor. The day I went there, you were getting off the elevator as I was getting on. We brushed shoulders. You didn't notice me, but I saw you. And I couldn't seem to forget you. I even dreamed about you. And then when I went to San Miguel, there you were…" She trailed off. "That day in the elevator…was it really just a coincidence?"

His gaze deepened. "Maybe. Or maybe it was just one more sign that you and I were meant to be together."

Anna stared up at him. "What are you saying, Ben?"

She didn't want to get her hopes up, but…what was he saying?

He took her face in his hands. "I don't care whose heart you have. It's you I care about. It's you I want to spend the rest of my life with."

Anna could hardly breathe by this point. "But… my condition…there's no guarantee how long…"

"I'm not asking for guarantees. All I'm asking is that you give us a chance. We haven't known each other that long. I realize that. We'll need some time. We'll take it slow and easy, and then when we're both ready…when the time is right…"

"When the time is right?" she whispered.

"I'll ask you to be my wife."

He kissed her then, more gently than he had ever done before, and Anna felt tears sting behind her lids at such tenderness.

She kissed him back, not so gently, and as his arms came around her and pulled her close, her new heart beat a steady, reassuring rhythm inside her chest.

A new heart. A new life. A new love.

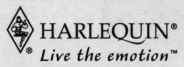

USA TODAY *bestselling author*

JULIE
KENNER

Brings you a supersexy tale of love and mystery...

Silent CONFESSIONS

A BRAND-NEW NOVEL.

Detective Jack Parker needs an education from a historical sex expert in order to crack his latest case—and bookstore owner Veronica Archer is just the person to help him. But their private lessons give Ronnie some other ideas on how the detective can help *her* sexual education....

"JULIE KENNER JUST MIGHT WELL BE THE MOST ENCHANTING AUTHOR IN TODAY'S MARKET."
—THE ROMANCE READER'S CONNECTION

Look for SILENT CONFESSIONS, available in April 2003.

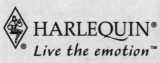

HARLEQUIN®
Live the emotion™

Visit us at www.eHarlequin.com

PHSC

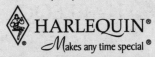

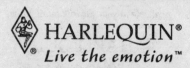